THE CURSE AT LILAC WATERS

THE CURSE AT LILAC WATERS

Anne -
Thanks for the
great Dragonfly - bead
class!
Enjoy the reading
Wilma ☺

WILMA FLEMING

Corinthians 13:13

This book is a work of fiction. Any similarities to real people or historical events are purely coincidental. The names of characters, their actions, or incidents are a product of the author's imagination, although some places and locales named in the setting of the story are real.

ISBN-13: 9781540607720
ISBN-10: 1540607720
Library of Congress Control Number: 2016919809
CreateSpace Independent Publishing Platform
North Charleston, South Carolina

To my husband, Norm:

Your real "boy" memories helped bring my story to life. Thank you for being the one I always turn to first, for help of every kind.

TABLE OF CONTENTS

PREFACE

As the only girl in the family and a constant reader, I was dismayed by the utter lack of interest young boys had in books. I wanted to write a novel that boys, (like my three brothers and their friends) would be enticed to read all the way to the end.

ACKNOWLEDGMENTS

My most sincere thanks go to all family members and friends who endured my endless questions.

To the readers and writer-friends in New York, Florida, and Pennsylvania: Your critiques with honest feedback stayed the course. Your friendship, help, and kindnesses are with me in every sentence I will ever write. You know who you are. ☺

Chapter 1

THE CURSE

Troelina was flunk-out lost. She munched on a breakfast of dry forage for the third lonesome morning and thought homesick thoughts about her tribe.

At the same moment and quite a distance away, as the goose flies, Troelina's boyfriend, Fole, was rounding up a search party.

"Find Troelina, find Troelina." Fole repeated as they searched through the dense forest.

Troelina was the most-favored troll within their little tribe. She'd had the good fortune of being born with a face more delicate than most trolls wore. The favoritism shown by the tribe gave her a sense of power and independence. If Troelina wanted to pick from the best blackberry bushes, she did so. When she felt like wandering away from the safety of her peers, she did that too. So it was no wonder that three days ago when she happened upon the old grisly goat called Krug, he'd challenged her.

⌒/|⟋⟍

"I'm feeding here, you simple-minded troll," Krug declared. "Go someplace else to eat."

Troelina did not take orders well. *Naagh, stupid old goat,* she thought and moved right past him, exploring deeper into the shaded hammock to search for a ripe grapefruit.

"Stop I order it!" shouted Krug.

Troelina wrinkled her nose and quickened her pace, ignoring him again. Further inward she went, where swampy vines tangled and the narrow path twisted in, then out, leading her closer to the river.

Troelina knew enough to watch out for the alligators. She carried her club as she had been taught. What she didn't know was she had trespassed over the border into Goatsland. And inside Goatsland, an alligator was not her biggest worry.

Troelina soon discovered Krug's complete herd. Never had she seen so many goats in one place. White ones, gray ones: they bleated everywhere, enjoying the greatest feast in the biggest, greenest field Troelina had ever seen. Huge berry bushes surrounded them, and the trees hung heavy with fruit. Troelina sniffed the tangy scents in wonder. "Wait till Fole sees!" she exclaimed.

Krug trotted up right behind her. "You'll jabber this to no one," he commanded, and before she could blink, he butted her from behind. Troelina stumbled.

"Garrumph, goat!" She said, regaining her balance. She snatched up her club, intent on swinging it, but the goat was faster. He circled around her on nimble hooves. With head low he bumped her again, harder this time, square upon her large purple rump. Troelina went flying. Her sweet little face was pushed down into the sand. She got up snorting, and just as she swung her club toward the goat's prickly beard, he spat out these strange, indecipherable words:

"Mitchkeet, Happ, StanzeGreegan Fooh."

Instantly, poor Troelina staggered, as if dizzy. "Motherrrrr!" She said, but it came out whispery thin. Troelina slid down, hitting the ground where a dark hole appeared from nowhere beneath her feet.

She dropped inside it, dizzily spinning, and slid some more, downward through a slippery, dark tube.

Peculiar neon-lighted creatures of red and orange flitted past. Just looking at them gave her purple skin a case of the creepies. Luckily, she slid by too fast for them to bite. Yet those bug-eyes stared hungrily at her, and she smelled an odd, moldy odor.

"Naagh." She gasped. She could not take in enough breath to shout out loud. The air stunk bad. She choked out a strangled cry for help. But there was no one to answer.

Finally, Troelina stopped. Her feet met solid ground with a thunk. She gave her head a shake to clear out the dizzies. A tiny circle of light beamed in way above her head. All the rest was dark. Digging and clawing, she climbed toward the light spot, squinting to keep the sand from her eyes. At last, she poked her head outside. Her whole body tingled, like a constant itching, only she couldn't scratch it. When her vision cleared, she looked down at herself, crying out in total shock.

"Aagh, mine Fole...naagh. Troelina cursed? Goat-cursed. Troelina cursed into a...to...a...gopher tortoise?" Troelina stared at herself all over again. She felt her creased toes, her hardened shell, but the real horror was her face, which was now an ugly-feeling tortoise face... with a...beak? She had no idea how much time had passed or even where she was.

"Oo-Glogs. Garrumph...Troelina goat-cursed!" She stomped her feet and wailed it aloud. No one came to her rescue, nor could she hear a single sound. Troelina was all alone and scared from being turned so brown and wrinkly. She moved around in a kind of daze, walking now on four feet instead of two. She plodded in a slow, awkward gait, without direction. What a weird place without feeling. She began eating many of the low-growing green things she dared to taste. And she kept resisting a terrible urge to just dig, dig, dig. So dig she finally did, hard and fast. At the end of her first tunnel the view was much the same. "Naagh." She re-traced her steps and started over again, going a different way. Poking her head out from the second tunnel, she discovered a surprisingly peaceful scene: a most beautiful lake.

Ooo-loo, she thought. *Naagh bad?* Poor Troelina was spent. She stumbled, yawned, and looked for a shady resting place.

Later on, in the final flicker-light of the day, before a sorry sun melted into ripples and the forest nodded off to sleep, a mockingbird, the well-known gossip of the entire forest, flew right over and landed upon her shell.

"Hoo-ha, foolish troll," she chirped. "You should know better than to trespass into Goatsland. Now you are cursed. You could find yourself crawling on the earth as a lowlife gopher tortoise, forever."

"Naagh," said Troelina. "Tribe find Troelina. Mine Fole find. Spring come; Troelina marry Fole." Sweet Troelina winced in pure despair. It pained her heart to think of her dear Fole. He was the strong, silent troll whom she loved more than anything. She swallowed hard, thinking of his deep-set eyes and the wide, toothy grin. How she missed him.

The mockingbird smiled at her pain. "Only one thing I know will banish a goat curse," she muttered, tipping her wing.

"Whaa? Tell Troelina. Bird, promise be: Troelina's berries go to bird-beak, evermore. Oo, tell."

"To break the goat curse, you must find and swallow the magic pearl. It rests in the center of the white blossom that blooms inside the giant lily pad. This special lily pad floats in the middle of Lilac Lake. But be watchful. Garr, the royal white swan is always on guard there, and he is powerful."

"Magic pearl? Middle lake?" Troelina repeated. "Naagh...foo-bird. Troelina land tortoise. Naagh swim."

"Well, then, you may be eating paw-paws in the swamp forever, Miss Troll-Cursed Tortoise."

"Blasten glogs," said Troelina. "Aagh bird stop. Bird hepp? Hepp Troelina find pearl?"

The mockingbird gave no answer. Instead, she chirped out a mean little cackle and flew away. Troelina stared long after her but the flippant creature did not return.

Darkness soon enfolded the day. Troelina pulled in her scaly tortoise head and all four of those short, chunky feet. And for the rest of that horrid, suffering night, she cried.

Chapter 2

THE TRANSPLANT

"Eric, get back here!" said Elsa, hands on hips.

Elsa was Eric's nanny, or like a housekeeper and cook all rolled into one, only she lived with Eric's divorced father, Ed.

Eric ignored her.

"Eric, slow down, or you're in trouble."

But Eric knew Elsa would not want any trouble. He figured she cared way too much about Ed and what Ed thought of her. She was a pretty good cook, especially with peanut butter cookies, and OK as a nanny. But he was a boy who was too big for a nanny, and he had no one to hang out with.

The whole thing was his mother's idea—to send him off to this isolated Florida forest. Eric hadn't wanted to come. His father had lived here since their divorce, so Eric was supposed to live with him (and now with Elsa, too) for the rest of the school year. When Eric didn't have school, he was allowed to find his own stuff to do, which was pretty cool, but without any of his New Jersey friends here, what fun was that? Eric didn't fit in. Not in his new southern school and certainly not out here in this God-awful forest. He was a transplant who felt like he was wilting.

So he teased Elsa. He hid from her, or he got himself really dirty, which she totally hated. Eric found out she had a disorder of some kind. Something freaky-sounding it was—something called automysophobia. Because of it, she cleaned constantly, everything, all the time.

"There, I got you now, you!" Elsa grabbed his shirt, and he was caught.

Eric panted. He was out of breath but ready to dash off again. Then, in a blink, he saw it. Something swooped past, and then, poof, it was gone.

"What?"

"A big white streak…I don't know…something. It just flashed by. Over there, by those bushes, but now I don't see it."

"With your wild imagination I'm not surprised. Next thing you'll tell me there was…a…a dragon, and then you'd be off looking for Pokémon. But we cannot. We have to get back so I can fix dinner. Come on. You can come out later to look for the white streak, whatever it is."

Eric gave up the tag game and followed her back to the weird old cottage. He called it that, whether Dad and Elsa liked it or not. It was monster-weird, more like an old hotel with way too many windows and balconies. It looked like early Spanish settlers might have lived there, when they first explored Florida on the river-boats or rode in on donkeys loaded with gear.

"I wish I could have lived here back then," he said.

"Back when?"

"When men carried guns and bagged the rattlesnakes and gators."

"Oh? Like you would bag an alligator," she said. "Tell me, Eric, what might you do with one if you caught it?" She laughed, so he raced ahead and beat her to the door.

"I'd make you cook it for dinner, with the slimy guts and mud!" he said, slamming the screen door behind him. His new sneakers squeaked on the clean tile floor as Elsa went to the sink to wash. He grinned knowing just the mention of mud could sometimes make Elsa queasy. He headed to his room at the back. It was big but kind of creepy. At night the live oak tree outside his window brushed moss-draped branches along the screen. When it was hot and sticky, which was all the time, Eric hated opening the window because he'd hear that scraping sound all night. The spooky noise made all those silly swamp rumors he'd heard in school—the ones about bears, trolls, or mangy wild boars—seem sorta real. He'd never tell his father this. He didn't want Ed to think he was a sissy. Or worse, Eric didn't want to get stuck helping him trim all those branches.

"Too much like work." He sighed, flopping down on the bed. He flipped on the radio, which was another annoying thing. "I got no computer. And no TV," he said. How was a guy supposed to survive here? The radio blared on the one—honestly, the only one—country station. Elsa seemed to love it. Dad tuned it out. Eric suffered.

He washed up quickly and decided to set the table. He'd win points with Elsa because she wouldn't have to nag him.

"Did you wash, Eric?"

He nodded, grabbed the plates, and glanced out the window. There it was. A big, white *something* flew right by that clearing again, toward the lake. It disappeared behind the trees. Eric ran to the door to look, but it was already gone.

"Man, I missed it again," he said. "Right after dinner I'm going to the lake."

Elsa shrugged. She stirred her fried potatoes as Ed came in. He started right in asking twenty questions until he was satisfied Eric hadn't given Elsa any trouble.

"By the way, Eric, are you interested in going fishing tomorrow morning?" he asked.

"Fishing? Yeah, I'm in."

It was about time he had some fun. Out loud, Eric said, "Dad, will you take the pistol? Please? There's some big white thing out there. I just saw it, and—"

"Whoa, the first thing you wanted to do was shoot at it?"

Eric sighed. Ed was a botanist. He made his living studying plants. Ed loved all living things, even the bugs that ate up his plants. Eric thought he was probably the only dad in the whole county who'd never shot at a rabbit or anything. Down here, these southern boys were raised tough. The guys Eric's age, like this Jerry Lee, whom he knew only slightly from school, had called him "city-soft." And they were right! Eric didn't like it, or Jerry Lee, not one bit.

Jerry Lee knew his way around wild creatures too. He explored the swamps and hunted in the forest alone or with his friends. And they all carried their own .22-caliber rifles.

New Jersey's concrete was Eric's real life, and he spoke with its stinkin' accent Jerry Lee loved making fun of. The other bad thing… Eric had no brothers or sisters, and now…well, since being here, he didn't even have his own mom. A nanny instead. He cringed to think what the boys at school would say to that if they knew. In public, he referred to Elsa only as "the cook."

Elsa served dinner, which saved him his dad's "killing-things" lecture. They ate in silence. Well, Eric did. Elsa and Dad talked while he thought about saving up his own cash to buy a .22-caliber rifle. Even if he could save it, his dad would probably need to sign the paperwork. *Geesh*. He might as well learn to whistle Dixie, which, by the way, Eric thought, was one of the lamest songs he'd ever heard.

Finally, dinner was over. Eric skipped out on the chores. Elsa and Dad were gabbing away about some sago palm fungus, and didn't appear to notice him. He grabbed his home-made bolas from the hook in the shed and started off toward the lake. At least he had some kind of a weapon, even if it was prehistoric and awkward.

Except for a couple of chirping birds, there wasn't a stir outside. A citrus tang reached his nose and he breathed in deeply. Though Eric wished Ed were more of a hunter-type, he had to hand it to him. When it came to fruit trees, his dad grew the sweetest oranges in all of Florida.

He reached the lake and stomped around, making lots of noise to scare the gators away. Eric was still leery. In any body of water down here, reptiles could be lurking, just waiting for an unsuspecting meal to walk by. Jerry Lee said the gators were afraid of humans, but Eric didn't trust it. Once he'd scanned every blade of grass, he sat down on the bank. The sun hadn't set yet, but the sky was already turning rosy pink. He had about a half hour before dusk, so he stayed quiet. A great blue heron swooped in, landing only a few feet away. It started its stalking rounds at the edge of the lake. A few frogs started to sing, but when the heron snatched one up and tried to swallow it whole, there was a slight gap in their song. Eric watched, fascinated, as the bird gulped it the rest of the way down. He wondered what he would do if he was ever the food stalked by some hungry wild creature. Alone out here, it seemed way too possible.

An odd sound came from the lake's far end. It wasn't a gator's bellow; he could identify them easily now. He reminded himself again not to hang out there after dark. He scrambled to his feet as a wavy shadow netted over the trees, like a 717 coming in for a landing.

A white pelican? He loved their ginormous wingspan. *Whoa.* Something else was swimming over there. It kept close to the reeds. Maybe it was only...floating? The shape was hidden by low hanging moss and stuff, but it looked big. Eric stayed still, squinting, trying to see more clearly through the snarled vegetation. The distant jangle of Elsa's bell sounded, prompting him to go home.

"Oh, rats." He'd have to scout about later, maybe tomorrow after the fishing trip. Whatever the "white thing" was out there, he would see it eventually. After all, he had the rest of this whole brutal year to look.

Chapter 3

SEARCHING

A skinny gray squirrel perched high on an oak limb snapped his tail back and forth, back and forth. Shiny black eyes sighted a drooping branch nearly five feet away. With an athletic leap, he spanned the distance. His front paws held, and he pulled himself topside.

"Good morning," he called.

"Good, aagh?" snapped Troelina.

The squirrel did not know how to reply to such rudeness. He came from cheerful stock and had been taught to respect strangers.

He tried again, jumping down and scampering near the tortoise's hole. "The wind is light, and nuts are plentiful."

"Troelina eat paw-paws," she mumbled.

The squirrel blinked, ran behind her, and scooted down inside her tunnel to look for something edible. A fat, smelly armadillo was asleep there, blocking the entrance to a second tunnel. He raced back up. "If I find any paw-paws, I'll tell you where they are," he said.

"Wait, Oo-glogs…" Troelina sputtered. "Squirrel swim?"

"I suppose I could," he said, scampering away. He did not wait to see why she asked.

Troelina mulled her question over. Had she ever seen a squirrel swim? She could not picture it. "Duck," she muttered, chewing another tasteless blade. "Duck swim."

The squirrel went on his merry way, making a mental note to investigate her second tunnel later, when the armadillo had taken his leave.

The forest surrounding Lilac Lake was bustling this bright warm morning. Fish surfaced in search of flies, and deer pranced to the water's edge to drink. Sandhill cranes conversed among themselves, punching long sharp beaks at random into the pungent earth.

Far away on much higher ground, trudged Fole. Back at home again he was unhappy to report no trace of his Troelina had been found.

From early human folklore it was told that the purple trolls originated from a mountainous Eastern kingdom, one sometimes called Krozerta. It was a common horde once found in many parts of the world. Several generations ago, however, Troelina's tribe had been isolated deep within this Florida forest by a sweeping wildfire. Now her purple troll family neared extinction. No newcomers for possible mates had appeared in years. In fact, only thirty-seven purple trolls remained. About a third of them were advancing in age. Their kind was the smallest of trolls in size, but being fairly intelligent, they'd adapted well to their surroundings. Wild boars, panthers, alligators, or snakes posed serious threats. However, the humans and goats were the worst invaders. The humans now inched further down upon them from the north, while Goatsland crept in ever closer on the west. The trolls instinctively kept distant from humans, although they learned many things from observing them, especially with tools or language skills. With such dwindling troll numbers, they discovered it was not the two-legged humans who posed their greatest danger. It was the goats. One goat in particular could ruin them.

Krug was this feared goat enemy. He had rounded up a sizable herd, most of them stolen from the human settlers. Over time, as his herd grew larger, he kept control by moving them deeper into forest hiding. Eventually he sought to drive out the trolls and take their land for himself. Krug brought another evil to the forest too. Somewhere in his extensive travels he'd struck a personal deal with a wicked, wily witch. The witch had given Krug a special power. He could now place a turning curse upon those trolls who dared to anger him.

It had happened on occasion (mostly in times of severe hunger) that a purple troll might catch, boil, and eat a goat from Krug's herd, *if* one could be snatched outside the Goatsland boundaries unseen. For inside Goatsland, Krug reigned supreme. He alone held this mysterious cursing power.

Fortunately, the truth of the trolls' weakened status had not yet spread much beyond their immediate area. Older trolls did not speak of it, for they feared the purple trolls, like Mesozoic reptiles in some old human book, would one day cease to be.

At random these days, an ugly-looking, ill-mannered goat might wander right in among them, just to make trouble. He ate the troll's food or butted them away from their shade trees. Most trolls gave him plenty of space. He was, after all, one of Krug's nephews, and none dared to boil him, for fear of Krug's wrath. It was for this reason that Troelina's beloved Fole searched for her with relentless focus. For the past two nights, he dreamed his slobbery troll dreams, waking with a start in the moonlight, thinking he heard goats bleating and Troelina calling his name.

"Fole finds," he had assured Troelina's mother. But his close friends knew the truth. Fole was plenty worried, and it was Krug the goat who worried him the most.

If only Fole's search party had crossed over to the furthest meadow and followed it beyond the pines, past the most-secluded pathway leading down into Goatsland, they could have discovered a big hint. Troelina's club was still lying there on the ground, right where she had dropped it. Instead, the clueless trolls trudged the other way round, returning to their anxious tribe with a grieving-hearted, lovestruck Fole in the lead.

Chapter 4

GONE FISHING

The morning fog smelled like fish eyes and swamp bottom. For Eric, sniffing it in at 6:00 a.m. was not a problem. He was ready, more than ready, to get out into some open water for adventure.

"Where do we meet the ranger, Dad?" he asked.

"Well, Bob keeps his pontoon up in Leesburg, so we'll wait by the river till he pulls up at the dock for us. You want a soda? It'll get hot out there once the fog burns off."

"Yeah, thanks," said Eric, hopping out to retrieve the gear as soon as the truck was parked. From the videos he'd seen of Florida fishing, today should be an awesome day. He was excited, but also a little bit squeamish about his first pontoon boat ride in alligator waters.

His dad's friend, Bob, was a forest ranger and experienced captain, so Eric was determined not to look too worried.

"Hey Dad, shouldn't we have live bait on board?"

"I've got it; worms and minnows. Both guaranteed to get us a big ole bass interested in breakfast."

Eric grinned. He knew his dad was putting on his southern-red-neck-fisherman act. He sounded just as silly as Jerry Lee when he was trying to be superior. In fact, Dad was almost as green as Eric when it came to boat fishing. Elsa told Eric that Ed had almost fallen off the boat the first time he went out. They'd crossed the channel to Lake Griffin in this same pontoon, and Bob had taken him all the way through the locks, which connected the Harris chain of lakes to the Ocklawaha River. Elsa said Ed had told her when they got inside the lock the first time, the gate slammed down, and the water rushed in so fast that it heaved the boat sideways and he was thrown off balance. His wet feet slid, and he had to grab onto the rail to keep from pitching overboard.

It would be worth any amount of money to have seen that! Eric tucked the story away to remind himself; if that same scene happened today, he'd be prepared. Eric wore his hiking boots, and though his feet would sweat like a toilet tank, he would keep his footing, even on a wet deck. No way would he be lookin' like a pansy falling off Bob's boat in front of Dad.

Dad brought the sodas and was busy yapping with a couple guys who camped nearby. Eric set the poles down and sidled over to hear more of the conversation.

"No kidding?" said Dad. He pointed to a brown burlap bag lying on the ground. "Guess what these guys were catching," he said, looking pointedly at Eric.

"Um, I don't know," Eric mumbled, feeling his neck flush. Dad must know he wasn't up on naming Florida fish yet.

"Go ahead, boy," said one. His hair was all matted down from sweat, and he had tattoos on both forearms. "Take a look there fer yerself."

The guy raised an eyebrow, and Dad chuckled, so Eric un-twisted the neck of the bag, tugging one corner open to peek.

"Yeow!" He dropped it immediately, and jumped back a foot as a rattlesnake stuck its flat, ugly face out the hole and started crawling right toward him.

The bigger guy laughed, stuck out his boot, stepped gently on the snake, and then pulled both ends of the bag back up, letting gravity do the rest. That bad boy slid right back down inside the bag. He twisted it shut again.

"You ever bag a rattler, son?" he asked, grinning.

Eric's eyes were still poppin' out of his head. In slow-motion he shook his head 'no.'

"Well, it takes a lil' southern know-how to catch-em when they git this big an' ornery," said the other. "But if ya' ever do wanna' go out snake huntin', jest have yer dad give us a shout." With that, they slung their booty back into the boat, as if they had only a few rocks in that bag. Eric was glad to see them go. He might have talked real brave with Elsa about baggin' rattlesnakes, but seeing a big one up that close just gave him the belly-crawls.

Dad grinned. "Every tree has a different bark," he said.

Eric was about to agree when Bob's boat came chugging around the bend. *Oh no.* His insides groaned. As if surprise rattlesnakes were not enough, Ed greeted Bob, followed by a second welcome, to none other than Bob's son, Jerry Lee.

Once they boarded, Eric grunted a meek, "Hello." He stationed himself way at the back, hoping Jerry Lee might stay up front. He enjoyed the view as they moved along to find the first casting spot. His strategy worked, for about three minutes. Bob set anchor.

"Hey, Err-ric," said Jerry Lee, drawling out his words. "Ah didn't know they grew fishuh-men up in Pann-sull-vanya."

"New Jersey," corrected Eric. "Actually, I'm just learning to fish." He thought the comment might cut him some slack if he didn't catch anything right away.

Jerry Lee smirked and cast his line like an expert.

Sweet. Now he'll be watching me. Thankfully, Eric had fished a few times before, so he could at least cast his line in the water without a fuss. No lie, just having Jerry Lee standing there made him feel like a wimpy five-year-old.

"Aww right!" The line took a snap backward. Of course, Jerry Lee took bragging rights for the first fish of the day. He held it up, and Eric guessed it went about two pounds.

Ed came over and gave Jerry Lee's shoulder a shake. "A pretty nice bass. It looks like we've got ourselves a real fisherman onboard, Bob."

Eric nodded, but inside, his stomach felt like it was still in the bottom of the rattler bag.

Eric tried hard. Jerry Lee kept his smirk on for most of the morning. He and Dad kept a steady competition going awhile, bringing in four apiece. About ten o'clock, Eric checked his watch. He hadn't caught a single stinkin' thing, and thankfully, Bob had only snagged one. Eric needed a pick-me-up.

"Hey, Jerry Lee," he said, just loud enough for all to hear. "How are you at solving riddles?"

Jerry Lee shrugged.

"One night a king and a queen went into their empty castle. The next morning, three people came out. Who was the third person?"

Jerry Lee gave a bored look, shrugged again, and nonchalantly cast a new line.

Bob thought a minute and took the bait. "Must have been the cook," he offered, which made Dad chime in.

"No...the castle was empty when they went in, right? So they had to have been invaded during the night. I'd say it was a robber."

"Good guess, but you're both wrong." Eric grinned, enjoying this now. "So what's your guess, Jerry Lee?" It was Eric's turn to smirk. Jerry Lee didn't have a guess. Not one.

"OK, I'll give it to you once more." Slowly, Eric repeated the riddle. "One night...a king and a..."

"Oh, I get it now," said Bob. "It was the knight."

"Right," replied Eric. "That was quick, Bob. Last year I stumped my whole science class with that one."

"Well, riddle this!" yelled Jerry Lee, suddenly yanking his right arm up hard, setting a tight line. They glimpsed one big fish at first splash. All thoughts of riddles or any other mind games were gone with the wind. Everyone reeled in their lines, and Ed grabbed the net. Bob started coaching for the fight.

"Set your drag a little tighter, that's it," he said and then, "Watch him...he's going down."

Everyone enjoyed the thrill of the fish fight a few minutes, watching the water sparkle around that single string, staring hard into the deep, hoping for another look at the mystery fish. Eric wondered what tricks he'd try next to shake himself free of the hook.

"What'd you have on when he struck?" asked Ed.

"A good-sized minnow; mebbe four inches."

The fish surfaced once, dove down again, and sent a rapid "V" through the water, trailing on over to the right side, where some vegetation poked up.

"Don't let him get into the weeds," cautioned Bob.

It was exhilarating action, and though Eric hated to admit it, Jerry Lee did an admirable job. He tired the fish out and landed the bass, all five pounds, six ounces of one beautiful large-mouth.

Problem was Jerry Lee's mouth was bigger than the fish's. Eric heard every fish story he knew, all the way back. They docked for lunch at 11:30 a.m., and Eric couldn't believe five hours had gone by so fast. He also couldn't believe he was the only one with no catch. *I'm such a loser.*

The ride home was quiet. Even though Bob invited them both for a trip to the Everglades National Park the next week, Eric couldn't get too excited. Not another adventure with Jerry Lee! He was thinking he might have to come down with the flu or something.

Dad tried to cheer him up, offering to stop for ice cream even, but Eric wasn't in the mood. He could clean his dad's fish, though, so he decided to do that while Ed put the gear away. He didn't bother taking off his wet boots, although he knew it was against Elsa's squeaky-clean rules.

More bad luck. Elsa came sauntering into the kitchen just as he was cutting the head off the fish. Some of the fish blood splattered up onto some white lacy thing she had folded on the counter.

"How could you bring that smelly thing in here?" she said, her voice going kind of screechy. "You've ruined my tablecloth with your dirty fish slime."

"Well, I live here too, ya know," Eric spat back. "And I don't see your name on my dad's sink!"

It was a short-lived argument because she did something so unexpected Eric simply couldn't believe it. The color drained right out of her face and she started to sway a little. Then she dove head first into the sink and actually hurled in it.

At that moment, Ed walked in. He put his arms out to steady Elsa and commanded, "Eric, go to your room."

"But, Dad, I didn't do anything to her...she..."

"I said, *go*."

Eric stomped down the hall in his wet sloshy boots, leaving the fish head, the guts, and all the rest of it right there. *Let them clean it up. Elsa can freak out some more for all I care.*

He slammed his bedroom door so hard it rattled the mirror on the opposite wall.

Chapter 5

THE WHITE THING

Garr was a grand swan of a different feather. Beautiful, haughty, and silvery white, he swept through Lilac Lake's waters as if he owned every droplet.

In a curious way, he did. For Garr descended from the earliest royal swan families that had decided to break away from Europe and settle in America. Some of his original ancestors still remained in France and the Netherlands, having had no desire to leave their known waters for adventure in some rugged, untested place. For all Garr knew, he could be the only male royal swan alive here in this country. Not that Garr cared much about ancestry. Not a beak. But he did care about his father. It was from him he had inherited his family's strength and super-size. It came down to Garr for this special purpose: to transform his body and bring forth the next royal swan heir. Father said it would soon be time for this physical challenge, and Garr felt he was more than ready.

For several years Garr had guarded this magical lake with the superior grace befitting a royal swan. He lived large, not in a bullying way, for his father, now dead, did not like bullies. According to father's final instructions, guarding at Lilac Lake was only a small part of Garr's upcoming quest. He was to capture the magic pearl as soon as it appeared on the giant lily pad, swallow it, and allow its magic to transform his body. Garr could then bring forth a new clutch of silver eggs to carry on the bloodline. From those silver eggs, the royal swans hoped to have another male cygnet. The new cygnet would be strong, like Garr himself, to survive the hatching and might someday grow to become Garr's replacement.

As Garr swam around the lake again, he could not imagine how it must have felt for his father, a large male swan, to actually transform himself into a female, and hatch out those eggs. But magic was magic, and Garr needed the pearl to accomplish it. So he swam about this beautiful lake, checking upon the lily pad every day, just waiting. When the special time came, and the waters changed to lilac, the magic pearl would appear. He alone had been chosen to perform this amazing trick of nature, and the very thought of it made his feathers ruffle.

Garr bowed his sleek head, breathed in the gift, and swept his magnificent wings forward, lifting himself to flight. His thoughts returned to his father's final words.

"Remember, Garr, the magic begins at midnight, when the moon is full and the lake water bubbles up in lilac. You must act fast. You'll find the magic pearl with ease, for it appears inside the lily's center blossom. You are a fast swimmer, so pluck it up, and swallow it whole. Then go where the underground spring feeds the lake. Inside this hidden cathedral of mossy trees, your transformation will happen. Let no one witness your change. I know you can accomplish it. The royal swans must have another heir, and it's all up to you."

Garr landed and re-settled himself. He swam the lake's outer perimeter once again, his eyes surveying each grass clump like searching laser beams. He shook down bugs for the fish and pulled up a few tender shoots for himself.

"I welcome the magic. I will transform with honor," Garr declared. His words were whisked away with the waters.

Meanwhile poor Troelina tossed in a restless slumber. She dreamed of her darling, gentle Fole. In her dream he had caught a glimpse of her and shouted out her name. She had been found! She gave a "yip," and the sound of it woke her up.

"Whaa goat-curse?" she mumbled. As she came further awake, she examined the length of her body for the nineteen-hundredth time. Her legs had not grown longer, nor had any of her skin returned to its lovely purple shade.

"Naagh Troelina," she said as her sleepy mind worked out a bit of a plan. It was hard to concentrate without her Fole nearby. She missed him so much.

"Troelina get pearl, break curse, marry Fole," she repeated, as if he were right there to hear. Her predicament was so awful in scope and her solutions so few Troelina had a hard time staying asleep. Suddenly, another of her worst fears appeared, flying right past her face. The mockingbird landed near her head.

"Go naaagh." Troelina snarled in distaste.

"Well, I have some new information, but if you don't want to know it, then of course, I'll go," she twittered.

"Blastin' glogs bird. Hepp Troelina find pearl? Troelina naagh tortoise."

The mockingbird cackled. "I thought you might wish to know your lover-boy, your trollie-Fole, is around. Did you know he is coming? He has reached this very hammock, and he intends to find you."

Troelina gasped. Could she trust this foo-bird? "Mine Fole? O'Blast...see?"

"Well, no, I didn't actually see him. I flew by and heard all about it from the squirrel."

"Fole here? Ooo-loo! Hepp bird, lead Fole?"

"Lead him, oh no, no, no. I did not. I didn't know exactly where you went." She cackled louder. "You always wander around this forest so lumpy-grumpy."

Troelina gaped in horror.

"I do know this," said the bird, suddenly serious. "If your Fole or any of his sluggy-troll friends aren't careful, the goat will attack them and curse them, just like he got you."

Troelina was about to ask Fole's exact location when the snippy little birdbrain took to the air again, laughing hysterically.

"I know what I know," she called back, "But I only tell what I tell."

Troelina trembled in anticipation. At last. Fole was coming for her.

"Ooo-mine Fole." She whimpered, suddenly frightened by the mockingbird's warning. Troelina pulled her whole self in, as tight as she could go muttering, "Troelina get pearl…break curse. Troelina naagh swim?" over and over, like a bubble-bearded frog croaking throughout the night.

Chapter 6

SEARCH PARTY

Fole plodded along, his eyes intently focused on the ground ahead. His meandering mind would not stop thinking. How could Troelina disappear so fast? Why hadn't she left him a trail to follow? Was she hurt or...worse? Questions cut through his brain like a rabbit run through the undergrowth, but he had no answers.

For the fifth time that morning, he held his club high over his head as a signal for his searchers to stop. The sun was higher. Midday eats had passed. Water-poles were getting low — perhaps lower than his heart, which he hated to admit was "a-draggin' to foot."

His friend, Zag, came forward.

"Water-pole?" he asked. "River wide. Trees shade."

"Aagh good," Fole agreed, dropping to the ground. He felt as helpless as a caterpillar trussed tight inside its cocoon.

He watched them all sit, because he sat. Each of them were loyal trolls who followed the organized troll rules. Zag took their bamboo water-poles, found a grassy knoll and pried off the top plugs, so all could be refilled.

Trolls used the thick-growing bamboo for creating useful items, like the water-poles, a necessary tool in the Florida heat. Each hollow bamboo stalk was cut and dried, forming a cylinder that held about half an arm's length of drink. Fat wooden pegs, fashioned from the durable gumbo limbo tree were forced in at both ends, wedged tight to seal the vessels. The bamboo was then wrapped in a sling made from large banana leaves, which were surprisingly tough. Once the poles were filled, the trolls hung the water-poles from the waist by ties cut from vines. Some tied a second lash above the knee so it wouldn't bang around while hiking. If the water inside the bamboo got too skanky, they flavored it with an orange or lemon slice. Thus the natural spring water kept them going in the insufferable humidity, day after day.

Fole looked at his friends and sighed. Gorrie limped, having stepped on a sharp thorn that pierced his big toe. He filled his water-pole extra times to soak his foot down. The rest were content to snooze, though Fole could sense their weary frustration at not being able to uncover a single sign of Troelina's fate.

The trolls had roamed these hummocks for centuries, before the goats, before the swans, and long before the two-legged humans appeared. It was their forest, and to lose one of their own in a goat spit, with no tracks found in explanation, was a pain not well taken.

Stubborn and deliberate, they did not want Fole to lose Troelina. She was special to Fole, yes, but also to her tribe. She was a favored female, though none would say it outright and risk Fole's jealous stare. If Troelina had not promised herself to Fole, any one of them might have tried to coax her for himself.

Troelina's hair fell in long, wild strings like tree moss. Against her purple skin, she wore a cover of woven-grass, as if she were one of the female two-leggeds and not used to going naked. She swayed in the breeze with a nice movement of her rump, like the eelgrass waved under water. A male eye was filled just watching her, then tongue-stuck, until she broke the silence with her bubbling laugh. All agreed; Fole was a lucky one.

Only now she'd gone. No troll had part in her disappearance; that much they knew. The rest? A mind-muggerin' mystery.

Zag returned, passing water-poles among them in silence. Lornie caught a fish. He threw it up in the air like a bird. Fole, without thinking started the game. He reached up to smack it back using the flat of his hand. The fish flew again, and suddenly, all the trolls jumped to their feet, exhilarated, leaping about like the wee ones, not wanting to be the one who missed their turn at a smack. Gurgles, grunts and outright belly laughs erupted as the fish flew. Back, forth, up, and down it went, and with each smack, it flew a little higher or a harder reach for the next. Finally, it landed between two feet in the dirt, and the game was done. The one who missed had to wash it, and slicing it raw, they all shared a bite. The trolls were glad for some fun to brighten the mood and sat down to relive the game's action while they waited for more eats.

When the fish came by Fole, he would not bite of it.

"Go…back to tribe," he declared and pointed his club toward home. The others protested. Fole insisted again.

"Naagh, Fole promise. Fole find Troelina. Fole go…Goatsland."

At this declaration, they all stared, eyes wide. Not a whisker wiggled.

"Go aagh," he said, standing his ground.

Finally a resigned collective sigh was heard. Goatsland was off limits. The trolls gathered their things and lined up single file. As they passed by, each one patted Fole's shoulder, the troll's way of lending goodwill in a dismal situation. In leaving Fole's search, they turned east and without further comment would return to the tribe the same way they had come.

Goatsland. The other male trolls knew not to go in there. If Fole was going there, he would be showing clear defiance to Krug. Fole admitted to himself that this was his last, desperate move. His friends would wait for him and protectively guard the horde during his absence. The trolls and goats had a long history. Most of it was bad.

Fole had lots of ground to cover. He'd organized this search party four days ago. From dawn until sundown, they persisted, walking a wide line through tangled, thick undergrowth, damp with muck, alligators, spiders, and snakes. They'd found nothing. It gave Fole the creepies thinking of the places they had tromped.

Troelina was nowhere. Even Zag, their best tracker, was stumped. Fole could not believe his feisty Troelina had gotten herself so lost she couldn't find her way back home. She had her club and knew how to use it. She must have met up with serious trouble. Where?

He couldn't wrap his head around any accident that might leave her hurt or possibly even…dead. She knew the swamp; knew the dangers. He would stake it; she could and would defend herself. So it had to be the goat. Nothing else made sense. He had to find her.

"Find Troelina, Goatsland," he muttered, slogging ahead, straight west. His eyes searched the ground for hints of any hidden pathways beaten down by narrow goat hooves.

Chapter 7

DOUBLE SEARCH

Eric woke up slowly, remembering his comical dream. He'd slipped out early, hoping to get a good look at the white thing, before his dad or Elsa woke up. He came upon it near the lake, but before he could get close enough to see it clearly, he dove right in for a swim. In Lilac Lake? What a crazy dream. *Like I would consider swimming in alligator-infested waters.*

His stomach growled but he ignored it, thinking, *If Dad decides to ground me I might as well enjoy my freedom before the jail sentence starts.*

He got up, and dressed as fast as he could. He stuffed a couple muffins in his shirt pocket. He drank greedily but rinsed his juice glass and set it carefully in the sink.

There you go, Elsa.

At the door he traded his flip-flops for a pair of old sneakers and grabbed his bolas from the shed.

Eric took in the silence. Alone outside, everything was quiet and wet with light morning dew. The sun spun orange threads of light making the tree line glow in the distance. He hadn't walked ten steps when he flushed a flock of white ibis. Their curved pink bills stabbed like little sabers spearing fat grubs from the grass. The birds fluttered up, but after he moved three steps away, they landed right back in the same spot to start eating again.

"Yuck, not too appealing for breakfast," he said and rounded the orange grove, going down the third row. He loved the way the heavy, moist air condensed in his hair. Here and there the sun streamed tiny prisms through the leaves. Red, orange, yellow, and green all fused together in colorful little rainbows. He imagined each clump of grass held a hidden gnome, maybe waiting to grant him a special magic wish.

"I want to go back to New Jersey," came out, and he felt an instant surge of tears. He guessed he was still miffed from the "fish-cleaning" incident, but dang!

"Because Elsa is some kind of antidirt freak," he mumbled, wishing he could say it straight out to his father instead of to imaginary gnomes. For a few minutes he was mad all over again, remembering the way Dad had jumped to Elsa's side. "He just sent me to my room like I'm a baby." *Burn!*

Eric rounded the end row and stopped with a jolt. Two deer trotted down the path ahead, as if it were the most natural thing in the world for them to stroll along this man-made trail. He stepped behind a tree to watch. The deer stopped still. Two sets of ears twitched forward, listening. He wondered if he'd spooked them and was totally shocked when a big stick came zinging right through the air. It bounced off the rib cage of the smaller deer. She stumbled from the impact but then bolted ahead like a shot, her companion already three leaps away.

Eric ran toward them that is, he started to run but screeched to a halt again when he heard a strange growling sound on his right.

"Garrruuuumph." It came again as a weird purple creature jumped right into his path! It seemed as surprised to see Eric as Eric was to see it. Neither of them moved. For a full second, neither one of them blinked. Eric recovered first, spreading his hands outward, nonthreatening. "Whoa...um, OK there...uh, what are you?"

The purple thing narrowed his stare and glanced over to where the stick lay at the path's edge.

"Hey, nobody's gonna hurt you, if that's what you think," Eric said, using a gentle tone. He hoped this unsightly creature didn't have ten rows of sharp teeth lined up under those big wide lips.

The thing must have sensed his fear, because it jumped forward, and two fat feet landed square in front of him. Eric jumped back a step. It jumped forward again. Eric was ready to jump back again, but he caught a flicker of a twinkle in those dark snappy eyes. It struck him so funny, like they were characters bouncing around in the middle of some new video game. Eric couldn't help himself; he laughed.

The laughing surprised it. The purple thing half-turned, smiled, jumped back again, and this time it reached out toward him. He patted Eric's hand. So Eric patted him back. It looked square at him this time and gurgled. Eric laughed out loud it was so…totally…nuts.

With the ugliest creature he'd ever seen popping right up in front of him, he suddenly imagined trying to explain this to Dad. The very thought of it doubled him over in a giggling fit. Eric sat down.

Then the purple thing sat down. It patted Eric's shoulder, but now it was sort of laughing too, well, it was sounding out a "huh-eehunh, huh-eeunh," type noise, which sounded more to Eric like a braying donkey. "Way goonie," said Eric.

It copied him. "Waaa-gghonie."

A few minutes passed with the two sitting opposite each other in the middle of the path, laughing, patting, patting and laughing until Eric thought his sides would burst. He wiped a few tears from his eyes and took a deep breath, saying, "OK, I gotta stop. Tell me your name or something."

"OO-loo," it said, with another donkey-gurgle.

"Your name is OO-loo?" It sounded so funny, Eric almost cracked up again. But he didn't want to be rude. He forced on a serious face.

"I…am…Eric." he said and patted his chest.

"Aah em Aahr-inck?"

Eric nodded and gently reached out and touched the creature's chest.

"Fole," it declared.

"Fole." Eric repeated it and smiled.

Fole smiled back, and Eric noted a few teeth were missing. Whatever Fole was, and by now Eric was pretty sure it must be a real purple troll, he didn't seem too dangerous.

Eric, have you forgotten the flying stick?

He hadn't. The wooden club had been thrown accurately and had probably broken a few deer ribs before it hit the ground.

Be careful. This Fole he must be a real troll. A real, wild purple troll. Wow!

Eric remembered his muffin. He brought it out and offered Fole a bite.

Fole sniffed. Eric broke off a piece and put it in his own mouth. "Mmmm, mmm, good," he said.

"UMMAummagoott," repeated Fole.

"You speak English?" Eric was amazed. Had he somehow landed on planet Neptune, with an alien? Fole only raised his eyebrows and held out his hand for more. So Eric gave.

His mind suddenly went zinging forward. He wasn't sure his brain was computing, but he had heard stories in school about these trolls. The kids said they still roamed free in the forest. Up till now, Eric hadn't believed any of them. Who would have thought he'd actually run into one? He could not take his eyes away.

Eric guessed the troll to be maybe a meter stick tall, maybe a little more. His nose, as wide as Eric's ear, had black hairs that curled outside his nostrils. His hair was so unbelievable. It stuck out all over in short, uneven hunks. Eric couldn't begin to guess what kind of gel he might use to keep it out so stiff like that.

Duh, brainwave, it's not like he goes to the hair salon.

The troll occupied himself by licking his fingers, which were kind of greenish at the tips. But his skin…not just the crayon color, but the wrinkled look of it, like...like an old leather ball glove. *Or more like elephant skin.*

"Sorry, I don't mean to stare. I, uh, just never saw anything like you...out here, or, um, anyplace before," Eric said.

Fole said something that sounded like, "Aahgaa, nah-gaa." He began sniffing around Eric like a hungry dog, coming closer and closer.

What the bleepin' freak? Does he smell me like he thinks I'm some kind of troll food? Do trolls even eat people? Or maybe they're vegetarian? Eric had no mouse button to click.

He got up and dusted himself off, being careful not to stare directly into Fole's eyes.

Fole got up too, but he looked straight at Eric again with a rather slitty-eyed stare. "Troe-li-na?" he said.

"What?"

"Troe-li-na," Fole repeated, accenting each syllable.

Eric shook his head. He pointed at the orange trees and said, "Umm, how about some fruit?"

The troll stamped his foot. "Troe-li-na," he said again, sounding gruffer this time.

Eric pointed at the oranges hanging from the tree, reached way back, swung his bolas around, and threw. They sang in the still air and sent a few oranges tumbling right to the ground.

"OO-loo," said Fole. He scuttled over to fetch the bolas and the fruit before Eric could think of anything else to say.

He might look chubby, but he can move pretty fast.

Fole looked the bolas over. He sniffed them. He scrunched his nose a few times, to the right and then the left. A bit of slobber came out of his mouth, and he wiped it off with the inside of his arm.

"Fish?" he said.

Eric was stunned.

"If you're asking, do I fish with them? Uh, no," said Eric. He was incredulous. This scary-looking hairy dwarf, in pukey-purple skin, did not want to fight him or anything but instead was interested in his home-made weapon. Eric decided to be honest.

"Um, Fole, I never tried to hit a fish with my bolas."

"Mi-bo-luss." Fole pronounced it like it was all one word and added, "Aaagh, Troe-li-na?"

Eric could not guess what "Troelina" meant, but he was getting thirsty, so he motioned Fole to follow and headed for the lake. Fole followed him a few steps but then stopped, ran back to the pine tree near the path and picked up his club. *Oh great…now is he going to clobber me? Or what if he decides to follow me home…then what do I do?*

Wacky thoughts raced through his mind as the troll followed close behind him. Momentarily, he had forgotten about alligators. Not the troll. He yanked Eric's shirt, motioned for him to get behind. Fole raised his club high, as if ready to beat off anything that came their way.

Hey, I think he's protecting me!

Good thing too, because off to the side a young gator lay sprawled along the bank. The troll beat his club only twice on the ground, and that sneaky gator moved over to the water, slunk himself in, and swam for the opposite shore.

All right…this Fole-troll is…pretty bright.

The troll got down on hands and knees and washed off the orange he'd palmed in his mitt. He bit it open and ate it so fast, like, the skin and all. The juice ran down over his chin.

"Aaaghgood," he said.

Eric grinned. He remembered the dangers that could be nearby and he scanned every part of the bank, looking for anything strange but especially the white thing. Who knew? Maybe having a wild troll along would bring it out of hiding and he'd get a better look.

"Troe-li-na," said Fole, and this time he motioned with his hands, like he was drawing.

It was either a guitar or a woman. Eric ruled out the guitar and shrugged.

Fole repeated the hand motion and said again, "Troe-li-na."

The dude must have a girlfriend. "A friend?" asked Eric. "Are you looking for a girlfriend?"

Fole made a slight moaning sound.

"Wow…um, I don't know, I sure never saw it, um, her, I mean. You are the only troll I have ever laid eyes on…and man…you really freaked me out!"

Fole sighed. He scanned the lake. He took a deep breath, patted Eric's hand, and started off again. He followed the path leading around the lake and turned right, going where Eric was officially not allowed to go. His dad said that path went through the sinkholes and farther into denser forest, where bears or panthers were said to prowl.

Funny. He never cautioned me about trolls.

Eric glanced at the sun, knowing he should be heading back. The troll kept going, though, getting farther away, while Eric just stood there, unsure what to do.

"Hey, hey Fole."

The troll kept on, as if he didn't hear.

Eric debated whether to follow. For sure, Dad would be up by now. Mentally he double-checked how far he'd come away from the groves and how far it was to the other edge of the lake. He was certain he could find this same spot again. Maybe the troll would come back. Eric imagined himself home in the kitchen, saying, "Hey Dad, I met a new friend today. A real live purple troll."

His brain dropped back onto its stem. Sure. *Like, could he tell anybody about this?* Nobody would believe him, not even Jerry Lee.

Fole was way ahead and not looking back. Eric turned then and started back home. He took some comfort in knowing that, if he was grounded next week, he could plan to sneak around some more and look out for trolls. If they were here in this forest, they had to live someplace. And clearly, Fole had shown him there was at least one other one around, maybe more.

Eric got excited just thinking about a troll hunt. He also promised himself he was going to find the big white thing, whatever it was. Somehow he had to get out of the house earlier, and alone, without Elsa worrying about breakfast. He looked down and suddenly noticed his empty hand. His bolas…gone.

Oh, that thieving troll. Holy guacamole!

Chapter 8

THE STORM

The sky darkened. Ominous winds sliced through the palm fronds like a champion serving a tennis ace. The animals ran for cover to hunker down and wait it out, for Hurricane Jeraldinia was on the way.

Eric's mother had heard the serious storm warnings on the Atlantic City morning news. She called Eric immediately.

"Hello Elsa. I'm so worried about this hurricane coming; would you put Eric on, please?"

Eric immediately turned his back to Elsa. Ed's antiquated telephone cord would only reach a half a meter, but Eric stretched it as far as possible.

"Yeah, we heard. No, Mom, I'm not scared." Eric rolled his eyes. "Dad said those news guys overreact to everything. He said we're not exactly in the storm's predicted path. And besides, hurricanes usually stall out before they hit here because we're so far inland. It's the beaches that will get the worst of it."

Eric parroted Ed's words to calm his mother down, but truthfully, he was kind of excited at the prospect of seeing his first real hurricane. A big storm would have to be more exciting than getting his plans shut down by his mother. First, she absolutely refused his request for a bus ticket home (though she said she was terribly worried about him), and then would not agree to give permission for him to buy a rifle. Any rifle. She simply refused to send him extra money for any gun.

"It'll be the best thing for you to stick to our original plan, Eric," she said.

"You mean your plan to make me suffer this whole year, Mom?" he said in his fiercest whisper. He heard her sigh and pressed his point. "It's not like I have any friends here. C'mon, you have to understand. Having Elsa is not like having my real mom around."

His mom sniffled, and she finally agreed to talk to his dad, but Eric could tell by the way she cut the conversation short it was going nowhere, so he handed Ed the phone and stalked out of the room. *It wasn't fair.*

Outside, the winds were already starting to build momentum. Jeraldinia's evil eye was seeking a clearer focus, and when the power suddenly went out, she swooped down upon them with a pelting rain, followed by buckets of dime-sized hailstones. A terrifying screech like Eric had never heard before, something like a high-speed commuter train, echoed through the trees. The house was in eerie darkness, and to settle his nerves, Eric started a game of solitaire-by-flashlight, slapping the cards down hard on the table. Neither Dad nor Elsa seemed to notice.

Finally Eric could pout no longer. He had to find something to eat. Since the "fish incident," Elsa left the kitchen as soon as he walked in. She acted like he was some dirt demon to avoid. He was really tired of her silence.

Should I go hungry just because she plays shunning games? Eric rummaged around, slamming cupboard doors and grumbling about starvation.

"We have lots of canned food in there," said Ed.

"And the gas grill has a full tank," added Elsa, "so I'll be able to cook dinner later, whether the oven works or not."

"The best news is there's a new generator, so if this storm pens us in for too long, at least we have hot showers," said Dad.

Terrific. It didn't look like anyone cared whether he starved or not. Elsa just sat there, knitting away.

Outside, the hailstones hit the tin roof, clattering like a packet of lit firecrackers. All three of them would have to stay together at the center of the house. It was the safest spot and well reinforced from the strong beams overhead.

Elsa set out some pillows and blankets to use as padding, just in case the windows blew out. Eric guessed they were as safe as they could be, but by the second hour, he was pacing. He inhaled the last of the potato chips and played another game of solo cards. *Who knew hurricanes could be so boring?*

Ed was reading, and Elsa went back to her knitting. Eric listened to the storm reports on the radio.

"This storm has definitely changed its path folks, and is now apparently set to pass right through the entire state, from the west coast to the east. Evacuation notices have already gone out to larger cities like Daytona Beach, but believe it or not, some people have ignored these warnings. We urge our listeners to please take the police evacuation warnings seriously. The high-rise buildings could receive heavy damage. When a category two hurricane reaches landfall, those winds could reach one hundred miles per hour," declared the announcer.

Elsa got up and turned it off. "I can't listen to any more of that," she said.

Maybe she was getting scared. Eric was too, in a way, especially when the announcer said the storm's path had changed direction. "Do you think the eye of the hurricane will come right through here, Dad?" he asked.

"No way of predicting a hurricane, son. Not for sure. Guess we just have to wait it out."

"And pray," Elsa added.

Eric grunted. He believed in God all right, but even in the Bible they had floods and earthquakes. Protecting them against natural things, like bad storms, was probably a waste of God's time. He paced the floor instead, marveling at the mass of leaves and tree limbs already littering the driveway. Earlier, on the radio, he heard that when Hurricane Ivan came through here, the destruction was huge, as if a huge bulldozer had cut a clean path through the center of the county. It tossed every little thing aside, like houses, cars, and boats—even some people.

Eric was worried about the troll too. Where would he go to hide out from a storm this size? He wished he could tell somebody about meeting him in the woods.

Fat chance they would believe me. It would sound too crazy. He wondered if the trolls would dig a tunnel, or could they find a hidden cave? Maybe they would hide inside hollow trees. What if the trees blew down? The troll and the big white thing were the two most interesting creatures to think about, and they kept his mind from going totally bonkers. What if they all died out in the storm? He'd never get a chance to find out anything more about them. *What if we all die?* He pondered that for a minute, but it didn't seem likely. His dad had reinforced this house to withstand hurricanes the first year he had lived here. He was so proud of it; he sometimes called it "the fortress." *No. We have nothing to worry about.* Still, he was glad to be inside instead of outside right now. That whooping wind was circling around and around the house, rattling all the shutters. The sound alone would give anyone the spooks.

"Hey Dad, how many people died in that last hurricane?" he asked.

Elsa gasped. "Honestly Eric, it sounds like you're hoping for the worst."

"I was just wondering," he mumbled. What he really thought was, instead of sitting around here unprepared in the dark, he should have a pistol ready. But he didn't dare say it.

"Dad, you never know what could happen. What if everything blows clean out to the coast? What about looters? Or bears? We ought to be able to protect ourselves, I'm thinking."

His dad only grunted and went back to reading. When he looked up, he gave Eric "the stare." "I won't be changing my ways about guns, Eric. You know that. I know mankind has been hunting for food since their first days, and I don't blame them for it; but we've learned a lot more about eating healthy plants and the sustainability of human beings through vegetarian diets, so we know it isn't as necessary to kill animals to eat as it once was. And, while we're on the subject, I think you upset your mother by asking for a gun and for a bus ticket back to Jersey. If you don't think you can make it here with me in Florida, you should discuss it with me, man to man."

Oh, crap. Eric slumped in his chair. Why did Dad have to talk down to him like that, and in front of Elsa? How could he ever talk to him about anything? He always...well, he acted like a stubborn old coot. Just because dad's precious plants loved it here, it shouldn't mean everyone thought Florida was paradise. Eric changed the subject. "Can I make a sandwich?"

"Let me," said Elsa, getting up.

Maybe she was embarrassed by the hot tone of their conversation. He hoped so. After all, if it weren't for her being here, father and son could have some real fun, like kids and dads were supposed to do. Instead, it was always, "Eric, don't leave hair in the sink; Elsa gets queasy" or "Take your shoes off, Eric; Elsa can't take dirty floors."

Guess what, Dad? Sometimes, Eric can't take Elsa.

A sudden crash at the back of the house had them all jumping up at once.

Chapter 9

THE AFTERMATH

Everyone ran to the den opposite Eric's bedroom. Part of the shed roof had blown clean off and slammed into the back of the house, breaking out one of the bigger windows. Glass shards twinkled on the carpet. Elsa actually screeched at the sight.

"Never mind," said Dad gently, and he steered her back while Eric helped him deal with the mess. Once things died down a little outside, they went out to the shed together, got the window boarded up with plywood, and swept up the glass.

The little rowboat, which they had placed right side up and weighted down with blocks of wood before the storm, was untouched. The lawn mower, which weighed more than the rowboat and the wood together, had flipped completely over. It wedged against part of the shed wall that caved in when the roof blew. No question, another big mess awaited them here. But most everything was fixable, so long as nobody got in a hurry. Eric was relieved. *We're lucky just to be alive.* Under such awesome wind forces, their biggest loss overall was Ed's beautiful fruit trees.

The next day Eric watched his dad's face as they walked through his orchards. It would take some time before he could add up all the losses, but seeing his fruit trees in total debris really pained him. It made Eric want to cry when he thought of the mornings he'd skipped his orange juice. He would sure miss it now.

"Thankfully, we're all OK," he repeated, and the radio announcer also pointed that out. In the cities the picture was much worse. Traffic lights had toppled into the roadways, bouncing around and causing accidents. Some people died, others were seriously injured, and wrecked cars littered the highway. The power outage left food soggy in freezers and people complaining about having no hot water. Telephones were out because the wires were all down. In some of the mobile home parks, according to the radio, it looked as if bombs had gone off.

Here in the country, they were far removed from big traffic, but still, some of the animals didn't fare too well. Eric found two dead birds on the patio, where they must have been blown right out of their trees. He helped Dad drag a dead doe out from under a heavy limb, where she had been crushed to death.

The two of them spent the next few days with wheelbarrow and rakes, cleaning up. Eric had never worked harder or sweated more. But he listened and was surprised how much his dad knew about the growing and replanting of all these things.

"I've got blisters on top of my blisters," he complained.

Elsa was pretty squeamish during most of the cleanup. However, she went after the entire house and patio like a demon with her broom, mop, and household ammonia. It was crystal clean, but Eric thought it stunk up to the galaxy.

"I'll not have any toxic mold growing in here," she said. Eric figured the best thing he could do was to stay far removed from any place she was cleaning.

He finally got a chance to sneak down to the lake and scout around. The water was nasty, a thick, muddied brown, and the grasses were flattened. Lots of smaller trees had been uprooted, with clumps of sand clinging to their roots. He saw a few small animals and birds skittering around the lake's edge, searching for food. The storm had scattered everything, and he felt sorry for them. He dropped his pop-corn along the ground so they'd find at least one easy meal. He felt guilty now for his early excitement about the hurricane. Now that he'd actually seen one, he didn't care to repeat the experience.

All he could think about was the troll. Was he alive? What was he doing for food? Would he ever see him again? He had no idea.

Chapter 10

GOAT PLANS

The mockingbird paid the old goat, Krug, a visit. She reported the number of trolls who had survived the storm and ratted on the one who had found his way into Goatsland to discover the troll girls club. The news sent Krug into a hoof-stomping rage.

"Meggarroot," he said, pacing around. "The trolls will want her back. Then their whole tribe will come tromping down here to help break her curse. Unless I stop them first."

Krug jumped upon the largest rock he could find and began to scrape his front hooves hard against the rough limestone. The scraping sent out a strange noise, a vibration, like a squeaky marker on a dry erase board. It zipped through the air and traveled downward, sifting through the sand. In minutes, hundreds of ugly roaches crawled up from the ground, glittering from the built-in neon located under their thoraxes. Krug kept scraping away as the bugs gathered around his rock like a swarm of bees surrounding their queen.

Krug looked them over. He spoke like a football coach rehearsing a key play. His head wobbled, his beard twitched, and his ending words were full of kill.

Whatever stinging power these roaches had, Krug meant to use it against those trespassers.

"I've summoned you for this reason," he told them. "The royal swan must be the only one to gain the magic pearl. The troll stays cursed!"

The roaches glowed hot pink in excitement. When the goat dismissed them, the ground moved in tiny waves from their retreat. Krug was pleased with himself. His confident swagger returned. He could wreak havoc with a wish, and any foolish troll who felt the hot roach stings would gladly surrender. He smiled a smile so evil his chin whiskers split right up the middle.

Chapter 11

DUCK PLANS

Troelina struggled. She was not good with numbers. She couldn't figure how long it had been since she was cursed. One week? Two?

"Troelina eat paw-paws. Cursed evermore," she muttered. Then her heart went a bit flippy, wondering if Fole had given up hope of finding her.

"Aagh Mummy?" she moaned aloud.

"What's 'aagh mummy, quacka?"

"Who wants to know?" Troelina snorted in surprise at the intruder.

"Quacka, I heard you whining yesterday and now here you are, doing it again. Quacka curious, that's all."

"Troelina naagh quacka."

"Quacka-now, don't be mad. I'm Dilla. Dilla the duck."

"Dilla…duck? Dilla. Duck?"

"Quacka am."

"Ooo-loo. Aagh good. Troelina find duck friend. Duck swims, aagh?"

"Quacka-that. Certainly I do. Swim every day."

Troelina flopped flat on her belly, too excited to hold up her shell.

"Duck, Troelina lost. Naagh tribe, Dilla. Troelina goat-cursed troll. Naagh tortoise…Fole find aagh…"

"Quacka-hooley, stop babbling."

"Unh lost, Dilla. Troelina lost. Naagh find tribe."

"Oh, my…well, quacka-that. It would be unsettling, yes."

"Troelina naagh swim. Swim lake, find magic pearl, break curse. Lily blossom. Dilla hepp? Dilla swim?"

"Quacka yes, oh, I see."

"Dilla swim…find pearl. Hepp Troelina break curse? Troelina find tribe."

"Curse? Did you quacka curse?"

"Goat-curse Dilla, Troelina naagh tortoise. Troelina…purple troll."

Dilla's feathers fluttered. She waddled up and gave Troelina a closer inspection.

"Dilla, aaghgood swim? Aagh, pearl? Troelina naagh swim. Troelina lost tribe, lost Mummy."

Dilla shuddered. Her beady eyes stared hard at Troelina as her flat feet began to flap in reverse.

"Aagh Dilla, naagh go. Troelina hepp Dilla? Troelina warm nest, aaghgood."

Eventually, the pair hatched out a workable little plan. Dilla agreed to swim out to get the magic pearl for Troelina. Troelina agreed to guard Dilla's nest, keeping her eggs warm and safe while Dilla swam.

"It gets so quacka-boring sitting on eggs every day. And I get so hot, keeping them warm all the time, quacka?"

"Aaghgood. Dilla swim," said Troelina.

"I guess so, quacka…only…"

"Dilla swim. Aagh pearl."

Could a duck hold onto the precious pearl and swim back all at the same time? Troelina was not so sure.

When she asked, Dilla calmly replied, "Quacka. I can swim while doing everything. Except for sitting on eggs, of course, quacka-quacka." Dilla chuckled at her own joke.

Troelina's heart nearly stopped with joy. Dilla led her over to where the nest lay secluded in the reeds. Three darling eggs lay asleep inside. Troelina climbed gently up on the edge and suspended her shell right over them, looking rather like a two-year-old human child, with her butt balanced squarely on the potty. She carefully placed herself and did not move. When Dilla was satisfied, she waddled over to the edge of the lake and plopped herself in.

Troelina held her breath, not believing her amazing good luck. She watched Dilla paddle a few ripples up, but then her view was blocked by cattails. She raised her eyes to the sky and smiled in relief at the fluffy white clouds high above. Soon…so very soon, her frightful curse would be broken!

Dilla swam halfway from the edge of the lake to the middle, enjoying the freedom of the moment and quacking happily to herself. Garr noticed the intrusion immediately. The swan barreled out from his hidden place near the opposite bank, with beak open and eyes narrowed. Without so much as a warning honk, he lowered his muscled neck, grabbed little Dilla by the upper bone of her left wing, and flipped her up and right out of the water, where she summersaulted high into the air. Dilla was so surprised she didn't try to right herself but instead came down hard, smacking the water's surface like a Boy Scout doing a belly flop.

"Quaaaacka!" she spluttered, sucking in a good bit of lake water. She didn't wait to see if Garr followed but made for the closest shore as fast as her flippered feet would flutter. Once safely on dry ground, she hob-wobbled, quacking loudly in irate fury. Suddenly, she felt a new determination to sit upon her nest until all her eggs hatched out. Taking a break and making a new friend no longer seemed important.

"Especially with a cursed tortoise, quacka-quacka." she said to herself.

Bless Troelina. She did the right thing, even in the face of such a huge disappointment. She apologized to Dilla. She wished her the best of luck with her egg hatching and made certain she was unhurt. Although her heart was broken again in more than two pieces, she slunk away in silent desperation, her tears dripping unchecked into the earth.

"Fole naaagh kiss Troelina's lips evermore," she cried.

What she didn't know, of course, was that Fole had already made it safely into Goatsland, without seeing the ugly Krug at all. Her Fole was right now in this very same forest, and not so far away. If she had been able to howl really loud, perhaps, instead of whining in her sad, sniffling way, he might have heard her call.

Her Fole was that close.

Chapter 12

FOLE MEETS ARMY

Fole woke up in a silent, scary space. Blue moonlight reached through loblolly pine trees, throwing long shadows over his body. He was getting closer; he had felt it since finding Troelina's club.

Without thought of food, he took a long drink from his Waterpole and started moving. Enough light came from the moon and stars to show his way, but getting through the maze of another Goatsland meadow was something he'd rather not do by daylight. He was still the enemy here. For comfort, he slung Troelina's club over his shoulder.

He had not gone far when he caught the scent of water. *Aaagh lake?*

Yesterday, his search party discovered a previously unknown spring. Might it be the one feeding this lake? Nature's law dictated that large herds of goats, like all other living creatures, must center themselves near water for survival. Thus, Fole came quietly into the lushest, best-kept secret the goat herd possessed. One thing Fole knew for certain was that Krug's limited curses were not spent without reason. His Troelina must have come closer than she realized to making such a discovery. If she was here, he'd find her, but he needed time to search without the goat finding him. For Fole it was a simple choice to continue. Without Troelina, his life would mean nothing anyway.

His thoughts were positive as he picked carefully through more knotted vines. He stepped into a clearing just over a small bluff and was pleased to see the lake spread out before him.

"Aagh beauty," he whispered. The moon was dropping, but the fiery morning sun had not yet heated things up. All was quiet. So.Very. Quiet.

He tiptoed forward, getting into the shallow water when he felt something bite at his heel.

Fire ant? He glanced down to pluck it away.

Not fire ant. A mass of shiny buggy things surrounded his foot. They crawled between his toes. *Stingers?*

"Garrumph." he whispered, remembering to keep quiet.

Fole couldn't stop himself from itching. He grabbed his heel and tried pulling the bugs away from his foot. They leaped to his hand, ran up his arm, and skittered further, some jumping onto his belly. *"Naaagh."* He moaned a little louder.

Sting like bee! Needlelike jabs shot throughout his body. What were they, and where had they come from? Fole did not know. But it was impossible to stay quiet now.

Do something; get them OFF. He took a deep breath and splashed himself.

Not helping. These nasty bugs held on tighter into his skin. A pinkish light beam shone from them as the stinging area glowed hot. And ooh, how it hurt.

Fole slapped himself again, hard. Little pincers dug in, held on, like nettles in a sock. The more he slapped or splashed, the further the stinging current zapped through his body.

"NAAAGH. OFF!" he yelled. In his haste to back out of the water, he slipped, falling face down. Roaches went into his hair, ran down his face. He slapped himself again and again. He scrambled back to shore on legs glowing neon pink. Fole growled in exasperation. He finally flung himself to the ground and rolled his pain around and around in the cool sand.

Meanwhile, high up in the leathery leaves of an old magnolia tree sat the mockingbird, watching the show. She would have clapped at the end for such a great performance, but from her perspective, a greater pink glow was now coming from the horizon. She'd promised to meet squirrel at sunup. Besides, she already knew the troll rooting around down there would be sore and dizzy for a time, but he should come out of it alive.

She muffled a laugh and flew off, eager to spread the news of the new intruder to squirrel. Once the squirrel knew, the goats would know, and then, of course, the swan too.

"Isn't this just way too sweet?" she chortled. "First the goat curses on the troll; now Krug sends roaches for the boyfriend." Finally she would have some real excitement. She couldn't wait to see how it all turned out. And, she wondered, who? Who would get to the pearl first?

As for Troelina, she sulked alone down inside her shell. Her duck plan was such a dismal failure. Dilla wouldn't likely be helping her again, eggs or no eggs. Troelina's sad heart drooped. Her stomach cramped. Now in a seriously "fowl" mood, she came out to look for a bite of food.

Had Troelina known she'd meet up with that silly squirrel again, she would have gone the opposite way. She had no interest in visiting, but the nervous little creature would not shut up.

She munched her way through his pleasantries, ignoring him, until he chattered something about talking to a mockingbird, who had seen a large troll splashing around in one of the lakes. She snapped her head around, and glared. "What lake? Troll where?" she demanded.

The squirrel pointed and stuffed in another nut.

"Lilac Lake?" gasped Troelina. *Could it be?*

Could it possibly be the trolls had found this same horrid goat place? That Fole had found it? Were they out there, somewhere, still looking for her?

"Troll? Where?" she pelted the squirrel with more questions.

The squirrel shrugged. "Why do you care so much about trolls? Don't you know they could boil you and eat you for dinner?"

"Umma, um, good story. Troelina naagh like trolls," she fibbed.

Troelina listened patiently, and soon the squirrel flipped his fluffy tail and scampered away.

"Fole!" She screamed his name as loud as she could. She heard no reply. No matter. She was taking a hunting trip of her own. If any troll was out there, she would find him, make him hear her. All she had to do was get over to Lilac Lake. "Ooh-glogs, Troelina go lake." Sooner or later they would have to come to drink or wash.

"Fole was here," Troelina repeated to herself over and over. She started out walking that exact minute. She would circle the whole lake if it took her fifty years. She would shout Fole's name to the clouds until somebody heard. Somebody would hear…if not her Fole, then anyone. *Any troll will do.*

Chapter 13

THE WEAPON

"Dad, I'm stopping by Ollie's to get custard, OK? I'll meet ya back at the truck," said Eric.

"That's fine. I'll be in the hardware store," Ed replied.

Eric thought he deserved a treat after the heavy cleanup work he'd been doing since the storm. Truth was, he hadn't been into town for over a week, and it was even longer since he'd tasted his favorite chocolate-peanut-butter frozen concoction. He sauntered inside and got in line, his mouth watering.

He felt a tap on the shoulder. *Why? Of all people, why do I keep running into Jerry Lee?*

"Where ya been hidin', city boy?" Jerry Lee drawled. He was standing in line, his camouflaged shirt hanging open and his sun-streaked blonde hair all stringy and full of sweat. He still wore his usual insolent smile.

"Oh, just around home," said Eric, suddenly embarrassed by his button-down collar and neatly pressed khakis.

"You guys git bad storm damage over there?"

"Yeah, my dad lost a lot of fruit trees. What about you?"

"Whole damn barn blew in, and my 4-H cow got crushed underneath one of the beams. She was gonna be my blue ribbon winner, too. I just finished buryin' her."

"Oh, geez, that's rough," Eric sympathized. "I don't have any pets, but we sure found a lot of dead birds around and a dead deer. First time I was ever in a hurricane."

"Guess we're lucky to be talkin' about it, huh? Coulda been way worse. Hey, I was wonderin' if you still wanna buy a twenty-two. I know you ain't done much huntin' but I gotta sell my old one so I can buy me another cow to raise."

"Really? How much?" Eric couldn't conceal his interest.

"Jes' fifty bucks. It's the first one I ever had, an' I bought it at the flea market. She's scratched up some, but she shoots jes' fine. Tell ya what. Take her home. Try her a few days. See how ya like shootin', and if ya wanna buy her, jes' call me, OK?"

What would Dad think of this? Eric's heart raced. *Maybe…could he get a rifle into the truck without him seeing it?*

"Well, um, where are you parked?" Eric heard himself say the words, even though he knew he could be getting himself in really deep.

"Across the street—c'mon, I'll show ya."

He followed Jerry Lee out, giving up the custard idea. He glanced back toward the hardware store to see if his dad had come out yet.

Luckily, Jerry Lee had the rifle slipped inside an old golf bag, so it should be a perfect disguise. *If Dad noticed the bag, he'd just have to fib and say he was trying out some clubs. At least he'd have a story to get it home undetected. No sense getting his dad all mad unless he decided to really keep it.*

Eric quickly agreed to take it on trial. He hurried to the truck and slid it back behind the cab seat. His dad shouldn't even notice it there. The ammo went in his pocket. Then he climbed in, breathing deep to slow his banging heart, and waited.

Once back at home, he helped Ed haul the plywood and some bags of mulch out into the shed.

"Dad, how about we don't start on this project till tomorrow?" suggested Eric. "I'd like to take a hike out to the lake."

"Sure," said Ed. "And thanks, Eric. You've worked hard this week."

"It's OK. I wanted to help. But if there's another hurricane coming any time soon, I'm saying we evacuate, right now, and you can send me back to Jersey."

When Ed went back inside, Eric lifted the golf bag out of the cab. He slung it over his shoulder and double-checked his pocket for the ammo. *Still there.* He grabbed his fishing pole too, just in case he needed a reason to stay out longer.

He wasn't sure how far away from the house he'd have to hike, but he knew he didn't want Elsa or Dad to hear him shooting and come out looking for trespassers. Ed was religious about keeping his land posted.

He headed east, and went past the end of the lake on the opposite side, putting some distance between him and the house.

Eric sort of wished he'd asked Jerry Lee for some instructions. After all, he'd only shot a real gun once before in his life, and it was a BB gun. He watched some hunting program on TV where they loaded and unloaded a .22 on screen. It looked pretty simple. Still, he got a little queasy, thinking about holding onto a weapon that could actually kill something.

The gear didn't slow him down too much, but after what seemed like an hour, he set everything down to rest his shoulder. He was getting sweaty and thirsty, but he ignored it. He couldn't resist getting the gun out to take a closer look.

Jerry Lee wasn't kidding about it being scratched. But he knew it would shoot if Jerry Lee said it would shoot. All he had to do was figure out how it worked. He slid the bolt back and then forward again. He used his handkerchief to rub sand away from the chamber.

"It should be clean enough," he said aloud, noting how his hand shook retrieving the bullets from his pocket. The gun was a bolt-action single shot, the same gun he'd seen on TV.

"It's now or never, Eric," he whispered and took his first aim at a small tree trunk. He slid the safety off, took aim and "Blam!" The sound wasn't as loud as he thought it would be, but he jerked when it went off anyway. He missed the target, hitting a tree right next to it.

He reloaded. This time his hand was steadier, and at least he hit the tree he aimed for.

"Yeah, Eric, you can do this."

Carefully, he laid the gun down on the ground. He counted out the bullets. There were twenty-seven more. *Enough ammo. Take some serious shooting practice and scout around for the white thing.*

Eric picked up the rifle, loaded it again, and started walking. If he stayed quiet and moved slow, eventually something might offer him an easy target.

Wouldn't it be so cool if he could spot that white thing again? Not that he'd shoot at it. Not unless he got close enough to see if it was something he needed to shoot. He just wanted to discover what it was doing out here.

For the first time, he felt like he was a part of this strange land. Like he was in control and could protect himself if some wild animal tried to attack. It was a good feeling, like he wasn't a dumb, goofy kid anymore but a real hunter, out looking for some game. *Yeah. A real hunter.*

Suddenly, he snapped his head around to the right. Was something moving over there…closer to that rock? He crouched down, stepping slowly, watching the ground ahead, and tried to hold the rifle steadier. He took another step, and felt a needle-sharp prick in the fleshy part of his calf. *Cactus. Yeeowch.* He yanked his leg away and lost his balance. The elbow holding the rifle hit the ground sideways, and the gun discharged. "Pichew!" The bullet glanced off a rock. His shoulder smacked a prickly cactus, while his other hand scraped the air, trying to break his fall.

Eric, you big wuss. He was more scared than hurt, but his cheeks burned with shame. *Some hunter you turned out to be.* Dusting himself off, he got up, and that's when he saw it. An odd-looking, dark-colored creature it was, moving rather unsteadily, kind of lurching along. *What was that?* He wriggled closer behind a rock to peek.

"Oh-oh." He let out his breath. The lurching creature was a gopher tortoise. Rather, a wounded gopher tortoise. And it was bleeding down the back of a crooked-looking leg. *You jerk. Your bullet must have caught him. Look at that leg.*

For a minute, Eric watched the poor thing trying to walk. A sick feeling oozed through his stomach. The turtle looked so totally off-balance, dragging the leg behind. The shell on its back kind of wobbled with every step.

You did this, Eric…you shot it.

"But I didn't mean to," he mumbled, but his heart was banging so hard he couldn't hear anything. He couldn't think what to do. He grabbed the rifle, put the safety back on, and slid it down inside the bag. He threw the remaining bullets in on top and slung it over his shoulder.

Then he just…ran. He didn't stop till he was almost home.

Chapter 14

THE EVERGLADES

Eric walked through the kitchen in the dark. "C'mon Dad, Bob will be here any minute."

"Well, don't get your knickers twisted; I'm coming."

Knickers? Old people talk so funny.

Eric heard Bob's truck pull in the drive, and he was the first one on the patio, even though it was only 4:45 a.m. He had his backpack and fishing pole all ready to climb aboard. Jerry Lee was there too, but Eric figured putting up with Jerry Lee's pain-in-the-butt-attitude would be worth it to see the real Everglades. Besides, since he brought Jerry Lee's rifle home (and admitted his dad wouldn't be too happy about it if he knew), Jerry Lee, the outlaw, was proving himself to be very good at keeping secrets. He let him keep the gun till he saved up the rest of the money, which was being pretty patient. Trouble was Eric couldn't be sure he even wanted the stupid gun now. He kept thinking of the turtle, dragging a wounded leg around. He wondered if it had crawled into a hole and was maybe bleeding to death. Every time he thought that thought, he got a hurling feeling, like his stomach dropped down toward his feet. Then he would imagine himself stumbling through the woods with only one leg.

Don't think about it. He needed this day to go someplace else, to kind of get his mind off everything. His dad and Bob had talked about going down to the Everglades ever since Eric first came to Florida. He was ready now for some new scenery and especially glad for a day without Elsa.

I'm gonna get scummy dirty and stay that way all day.

At first Jerry Lee took over the conversation, giving details about the new cow he planned to buy. It wasn't a milk cow, which was the only kind of cow Eric had ever seen up close. Instead, this bovine would be raised for steaks, and, according to Jerry Lee, they would be the biggest, juiciest steaks that ever came off a hoof. He didn't get into the part about how he was going to befriend it, kill it, watch it die, and then eat it, which Eric was thankful for. Don't get it wrong, he liked a good hamburger, too, but as a young kid, he did remember reading *Charlotte's Web.* Maybe some of the storyline stuck. Personally, he didn't think he could make a pet of any animal and then greet it on the dinner table. But hey, he loved catching fish, right? He and Dad caught fish, cleaned 'em, and ate 'em, without giving the fish's life a second thought. *But you cannot know a fish personally.* Maybe it was that simple. You ended up doing whatever you got used to doing. Eric shrugged. He wasn't in the mood to think too heavy, at least not today.

Bob turned south onto the Florida turnpike. The weather was perfect. The talk started about an alligator's mating call, which turned out to be an interesting conversation, because Eric didn't even know that alligators came out of eggs. *Ya must have missed that one in science class.* He didn't let on, but it was sort of a surprise. He'd never thought about it before. He was getting excited to see them up closer though, because alligators usually gave him the total jitters.

The more I learn about them, the better.

Ranger Bob was like a walking encyclopedia when it came down to how such creatures lived, and not just alligators. He knew everything about birds, manatees, and fish, pretty much anything that lived in this whole state. Eric enjoyed the trip down a lot, and he learned some good stuff.

Thanks to Jerry Lee taking a sudden interest in the best types of hay to feed his cow or what he should do about the mold growing inside his new grain bin, Ed was kept busy talking, too.

They stopped once for gas, grabbed a few Krispy Kremes to hold them over till lunch, and got right back on the road again. In all, it took about seven hours to reach the main entrance to the national park. First stop was the bathrooms at the Ernest F. Coe Visitor's Center.

"Man, I gotta have food," said Jerry Lee, as soon as his feet hit the pavement. Eric agreed, so they left the gear and opened up the coolers. For sure they would be better explorers with full stomachs.

As they snacked, he noticed the different birds. These creatures seemed to know exactly where to land to gobble up a small fish, spread their wings out to dry, or zero in on Eric's potato chips. The crows took turns pulling off this stunt. One of them got so brave as to swoop down over the table and lift a chip right off the pile on his plate. Once he flew away with it and landed up in the trees, there wasn't much anyone could do, except laugh.

After lunch they headed out to Royal Palm to hike the Anhinga trail, deciding to save the fishing for last. Bob kept them busy, lecturing like a teacher on a field trip with his never-ending knowledge. Almost an hour was spent talking—or rather, Bob and Dad were talking, and the boys listened. Thanks to Bob, they learned about the "River of Grass." He really had no idea of the human threat to the ecosystem of the Everglades. Bob and Dad discussed at length the water problems that might ruin this whole area someday—all because the northern people traveled here by the thousands, just to live in sunshine. Whoever thought about the water? Suddenly Eric was ashamed. His whole life he'd let water run down the drains, and he never gave a hoot. Now, listening to them discussing it and being surrounded by this wild beautiful place, he got it. He was an enemy.

City kids like him might grow up to find they couldn't get a drop of clean water to drink someday, because they'd already spoiled or wasted it all. It was so weird to think of himself in that way, like a predator almost. The animals were doing what they were supposed to do. *It was the people who made the problems worse.*

"Nice gator," said Jerry Lee. Eric peeked over the boardwalk and saw a seven-foot alligator lying there, staring right up at him. A few feet away were three ugly black buzzards, and they sort of hopped around, looking for a dead fish or whatever scrap a person might throw. Eric gulped in his own silent guilt trip. *The turtle...again.* One of these vicious birds could find it and attack, maybe even eat it up alive. Here he was hoping he'd forget about it, but being out here, where the weak instantly became prey, the limping turtle haunted him. *When I get back, maybe I can find it. I'll take care of it, somehow. Maybe take him to the vet?*

Later, they moved on to Shark Valley, where they covered a few miles on foot, hiking the trails, eyes peeled in hopes of a rare look at a wild panther.

Nobody got that lucky, nor did he spot any Burmese pythons. Bob told the boys they'd become a nuisance snake in Florida. Some of them were brought here by people who got them in pet shops, and when they couldn't keep up with the snake's huge appetites, they just let them go, out in the wild. Once the pythons were free, they made themselves too much at home, preying on the small animals. "It upsets the balance of the Florida food chain," said Bob.

"People can't leave anything alone," Eric muttered. *Like me, shooting a turtle and messing it up for life*, he reminded himself for the umpteenth time. *It was an accident, but I shoulda had the safety on.* He felt glum. He got to thinking about his mom and dad. How they messed up his life by getting divorced. He thought he was pretty much over it now, but still he couldn't forget how much it hurt when Dad had told him he was leaving for Florida. *It wasn't fair.* Eric thought about Elsa too. Maybe he wasn't being fair to her either, just because she wasn't his real mom. He could tell she did like his dad. Maybe she couldn't help it if she had a few goofy hang-ups. Maybe he was getting tired. He was relieved when Dad and Jerry Lee turned back from yet another new trail.

"We'll be eaten alive by the mosquitoes breedin' in there," said Jerry Lee. He whapped his hat down the full length of his jeans, trying to get rid of the bugs flying around him by doing a hop-skip sort of a dance. Everyone laughed and decided to head back to fish. Bob and Jerry Lee bet on who would get the first fish. Boating through new waterways was a real thrill, and fishing from Bob's boat was even better. Back home Eric had always fished along a dock or bank, but of course, back home he didn't worry about alligators or poisonous snakes.

He decided it didn't matter who was first, or even if he caught anything. It was all about being out here with the guys. To make it to their rental cabin for the night, they'd have to be off the water soon. The next day their plan was just to enjoy the outdoors some more and be home by bedtime. Nobody said much. They just fished, munched, and watched the birds. Eric liked the way the guys joked around and ate, ate again, then ate some more. It was totally awesome, and the time disappeared way too soon.

When they did arrive home, it seemed to Eric like they'd just left the Everglades and were pulling back in the driveway. He must have conked off snoring on the way home and missed some of the ride.

"It sure was a super trip," Eric said, thanking Bob again. *The best.* He carefully lifted two fish out of the cooler, feeling good he'd finally out fished Jerry Lee, if only by one. Eric also had the good sense to clean and wrap it on site, so there would be no Elsa problems tonight.

Eric said his good-byes and tiptoed into the house. Dad was beat. He headed for the shower, but Eric stopped by the fridge. *Milk and cookies time.*

He'd taken only a bite when he heard Elsa's slippers flipping along the tile.

"Hi, Eric," she said, smiling pretty sweet.

"Hey," he answered. From out of nowhere, they started talking to each other. Eric told her about catching his fish. But then he stopped, took a quick breath, and plowed in again.

"Elsa, I'm sorry about the fish mess I made last time. I cleaned mine already, so they're all wrapped and in the freezer. You won't have to worry about it."

She looked surprised, but a soft smile came into her eyes.

"Um, well, Dad's done in the shower, so, guess I'll get cleaned up. See ya tomorrow," he said.

"Thank you, Eric," she kind of whispered, but she smiled again, a real Elsa smile.

Eric had a good feeling that when he got up tomorrow, maybe, things would be more like normal with her.

Chapter 15

FOLE'S DISCOVERY

Fole dragged his tired, swollen body down to the water to drink. The stings from those horrid bugs made his purple skin all puffy and sick-looking. His feet got the worst of it, as they were glowing with bugs by the time he found the good sense to sit down. Every step burned. By afternoon, he dug himself a hole and put his feet and legs completely inside it, cooling them with milk from an aloe plant and cool, wet sand. Ooh, he itched! The trouble was when he scratched, the burning sensations came back. He tried to sleep, but the temptation to scratch was maddening. He knew he should get his head together. He would have to find his way back to the tribe. After he recovered, he would return with his friends and do a more thorough search.

"Agggh. Go naagh Troelina." He sighed. He was not defeated. No. Instead, the ugly roach attack left him angry and that much more determined.

"Fole find Troelina," he muttered over and over to himself. If there was a way, he would keep to it. He'd been crazy to try it alone. No use waiting. He would find some food for tonight and go back.

Fole rose, ignoring his sore stiff body. Carrying Troelina's club and his own, he knew he must smack a fish to get the strength needed to keep going. He stepped carefully around the water, like a heron stalking the shallows. Fole held his breath and stared. His trained eye soon caught movement—a carp, maybe—but he wasn't in close enough to smack it. He took another step, breath held, clubs ready.

Whaa? There was…something there on the bank, a short, dark shadow moving toward him…only a few feet away. *Oo-loo, was he in luck?* A tortoise. It crawled—no, wobbled—directly toward him. It did not appear frightened of him standing there. Fole held perfectly still. *Aaagh tortoise. Make soup for belly.* As the wobbling creature came closer, he raised both clubs a tiny bit higher. He crouched down, ready to smack it, first with one club, then the other. But the tortoise raised its head and did a most curious thing. It looked straight into his eyes and screeched out his name.

"FO-O-O-OLE!"

He gasped. That voice…it sounded like…but, no…he'd never heard a tortoise speak. And why was it calling his name? He stood in a half trance, staring. The tortoise lifted itself higher off the ground. It scuttled right toward him and called out his name again, fainter this time, but yes, clear.

"I am Fole," he stammered.

"Fole, Oo-loo Troelina!"

Instinctively, Fole backed up. The tortoise moved closer. He hit a bank and slid down, his rump landing not so gently on a soggy clump. He set the clubs down. He stared, unable to believe what his own eyes told him. The tortoise kept on. It crawled right up into his lap. He stared into those dark, strange eyes, and then, he knew. It was her.

"Troe-troelina?" he stuttered.

She sobbed then, burying her head down into his chest.

Awkwardly, he held her by the shell's edge, trying to understand. "Goat…curse?" he finally asked.

She nodded. Her speech came soft between sniffles. "Troelina lost. Goat-cursed. Fole find. Troelina love Fole." And she smooched her flat tortoise mouth right onto his lips. He jerked back in a little shudder; he couldn't help it. Kissing a tortoise? It was too much to take in.

For a long while, they sat together on that soggy bank. Troelina told Fole everything. It soothed him, hearing her voice. Fole relived his own loss, the long search, the stinging roaches, even his shock at finding her now, hidden within the tortoise shell. He cleaned her leg wound, smeared it with aloe, and wrapped it snugly in large, damp leaves. He tied it gently so she would have some forward thrust. She put her weight down on it.

"Back to trolls," he cried.

"Ooh, Troelina naagh go. Tortoise." she wailed, thinking of her poor mother, how she would feel to see her daughter cursed. She cried again. Fole gently rubbed her tears away with his thumb. "Fole break curse," he said. "Aagh trolls hepp."

The rest of the night they talked, exploring every possible action until they formed a brand-new plan.

"Oo-loo. Fole find Er-rinck. Go boat," he said.

"Fole find Er-rinck. Boy hepp Fole?" Troelina asked, still uncertain.

Fole had given careful thought to every detail.

It was Troelina who yawned first. She was so tired but also over-joyed. She was found! And with Fole in charge, her crying time was over. She trusted Fole completely. Troelina promised him she'd be brave, for in her mind, his new rescue plan with her curse broken was almost as good as done.

"Boo-ya, those goats will boil!" she whispered in fierce bravado.

Chapter 16

KIDNAPPING?

Eric was stretched out on the bed, reading about the strangler fig trees growing in the Everglades when something hard hit the window. He ignored it.

Ping. Ping! The window again, twice this time. He got up, tapped his bedside light to dim it, and looked out the window.

Nothing there...*hmm*...he glanced over by the shed and nearly jumped out of his curly brown hair. *The troll!*

As if he visited every night, there was Fole calmly waving away, motioning for Eric to come outside.

Eric waved back. *OK.*

He grabbed his hood and shut off the light. Slipping into sneakers, he went quietly down the hall, in case Dad or Elsa was still awake. At the back door, he grabbed the flashlight from the top of the refrigerator.

It was a breezy night but not cold. He didn't turn the flashlight on until he was almost at the shed door.

"Fole?" he called in a loud whisper. "Are you there?"

When Fole stepped toward him, Eric jumped, even though he knew Fole was there. It was just so weird looking at a troll, and in the faint light of a pale moon, he looked supernatural.

Fole grunted. "Aagh."

"Whassup?" asked Eric.

Fole pointed. He was hidden from the house as he stood in the shadows behind the shed.

"Holy crap-pola!" It came out sounding just like Jerry Lee, but Eric couldn't believe what he was seeing. The tortoise he shot on that horrible, awful, no-good day was right here and staring straight at him.

"Oh my gosh Fole, how'd you find it? It's wounded, and it's all because of me…I didn't mean to hurt it, really. I fell down, and the gun was loaded, and…" he stopped. *The tortoise was speaking to him.*

"Whaa-wha'd you say?" he asked, dumbstruck.

"Err-rinck," it sounded like.

"Umm, yes," Eric replied. "Um, I'm so glad you're OK. I didn't mean to run away and leave you hurt, it's just that…" He was yammering. *Idiot.* His heart pounded, and he was feeling really bad in his stomach again, plus, he had more than a hundred questions to ask.

"Err-rinck come?" The tortoise was talking again. It wobbled over to the shed door, which Fole was pulling on. Eric flipped the latch and opened the door for him, thinking they should go inside where they couldn't be heard.

"Boat," said Fole, gleefully, as if he were a human kid bumping into Santa Claus.

"Boat!" echoed the tortoise, likewise excited.

"Boat?" repeated Eric, still reeling from seeing (and hearing) this talking tortoise. *Can we please just get real?* "What…um, you guys want to take a boat ride?" he asked and then pinched the inside of his own wrist to be sure he wasn't dreaming or something.

"Come, Err-rinck," Fole said, but it wasn't a question.

Maybe his survival skills were kicking in as his brain started to fire. *What's going on here? Why do they want the boat? My father's boat. And where do they think we'll be going with it?*

Fole placed a hand on Eric's forearm.

"Hepp," he said. "Err-rinck hepp Fole." And he moved the rakes and shovels away from the boat, as if to…

"But…but it's nighttime," Eric heard himself protest. His mind raced ahead, mostly scared into the negative, but someplace deep inside, he was also getting a little excited. Could this be the wildest adventure ever? *Been complaining of boredom again, Eric? Well, haven't you?*

Yes, in fact, he had. But he'd never imagined anything like this happening.

Fole grabbed the bow of the boat and gave it all he had, trying to pull it toward the door. The boat refused to budge.

"Hey, wait," said Eric. Yet, before he knew it, he was dragging the front, Fole had the back, and they were tipping it sideways to fit it through the door. They set it down on the grass, and Fole made paddling motions.

"Oh, right," Eric said, and he went back for the paddles. As an afterthought he grabbed the life preserver he always wore fishing. *Were they going fishing?*

"Hey, um…Fole. You do know that alligators are out hunting at night, right? I mean, nobody, nobody fishes this late, unless…"

"Naagh fish naagh."

"Err-rinck hepp Fole," the tortoise repeated, running all the words together as one.

"OK, I get it. You want help. But help with what?" Eric felt his inner windshield start to crack. "You need help to paddle the boat? OK, I guess, so…but umm, where are we going?"

Oh, great…had he really just said "we"?

The troll put the paddles in, sniffed around the life jacket, and placed it inside. Fole lifted the tortoise up, set it gently in the bottom, and grabbed the rope. It pulled fairly easy now, so he started pulling through the wet grass.

"Um, Fole? Where now…where are you going?"

"Boat aaghgood. Errinck hepp Troelina."

"Troelina?"

Fole stopped. He patted the tortoise on the head. "Troe-li-na," he said.

So this was Troelina? The troll had a pet. A pet tortoise?

Eric was stumped. If Fole knew that he was the one who had shot his pet tortoise, why wasn't he mad? And what did the two of them want him to do now, with his father's boat, out here, in the dark, and...*what the hey?* What was he doing out here with nothing but a flashlight, and going down to the lake with them? *At night? Eric, are you stupid?*

"Fole, stop! Let me get the rifle. Wild animals are out here, wandering around Lilac Lake at night." Eric's eyes were already jumping out of their sockets. *Was he nuts to follow them?* Eric didn't know, but he knew he didn't have any weapon. He turned and started back toward the shed. Wild trolls might traipse around forests at night with nothing but clubs, but humans did not. He'd definitely take the rifle.

Suddenly, Fole tackled him from behind. Eric went down with a thud. His breath whooshed out, and his right knee grazed something hard. *What the?*

"Err-rink come," stated Fole, lying spread eagled in the middle of his back, pinning him down.

"Let me up!" Eric growled.

"Err-rinck boat," said Fole, refusing to move.

"Look Fole, you don't understand. Yes. I will help you with the boat—I will. But I need to get the rifle, for protection. Remember alligators? And by the way...you...you took my bolas!"

"Aagh. My bow-luss aaghgood."

"Good, yeah. But mine, not Fole's. Will you please let me up, because we need to take a weapon, or I'm not going anywhere."

Fole stayed put a couple more seconds and then rolled off.

Eric got up, dusted himself off, and started back for the rifle. Fole shadowed him like a second skin.

"Err-rinck come," he commanded.

"I'm going to come, yes." *This...this crazy, unpredictable troll. Could he trust Fole, like really trust him? Or would he try to take his rifle this time—and the boat, like he'd taken the bolas?*

One thing was certain: Eric would be on the alert. He must be extra careful. It was possible Fole wanted revenge somehow, because he shot the tortoise. Whatever Fole had planned, Eric knew, he had to stay ready. He'd also have to get right back here before sunup, or he'd have a lot of explaining to do. *This whole scene is way too bizarre-o.*

In spite of himself, Eric grinned. He could only imagine trying to explain this sneaky behavior. He didn't even know what crazy kind of adventure he was in for...not yet, anyway. But he was in. Oh, yes, all in. He really didn't have much choice.

Chapter 17

THE TIME NEARS

For days now, Garr had been on high alert. The tension surrounding him was so static his feathers fluffed further away from his body, making him appear even larger than he already was.

He'd chased every rabbit, squirrel, and mole away. He wanted this secluded spot all to himself when his egg-hatching time came. He thought the best way to keep it clear was to forcibly claim it well in advance. Garr was prepared and ready.

Still, the final hours were tense. Back and forth he swam, watching but not seeing. His transformation time was so close he could sense it. With regal head high, he waited, swam, sighed, and waited some more. The clutch had been firmly constructed and was well hidden in the reeds at the deepest indentation of the shoreline. When his body changed and the eggs came forth, Garr would deposit them there, where they would be safe until the hatching time.

For the hundredth time, he looked skyward, judging the height of the stars and sensing the wind. He wished for another sign, but the hour was late. He awaited the moonlight, the magic, and the deep-lilac coloring of the waters.

On the opposite side of the lake, Eric, Fole, and Troelina stopped for a short rest. They'd pulled the boat along the grass, Eric and Fole taking turns with the rope, while Troelina rode inside. At one point, Fole insisted on going straight through a small depression, which was filled with some dank-smelling muck. Eric's foot sank way down in, and when he pulled it out, the nasty gunk squished around in his sock, making him gag from the smell. For all he knew, it was an old sinkhole, and they might all disappear.

Fole didn't mind. "Er-rinck come," he said.

"Excuse me, but we humans like to keep our feet dry," Eric hissed.

Fole seemed to think everything Eric said was amusing. He grinned, gurgled, and kept on going.

If I didn't know better, I'd think Fole was related to Jerry Lee. He has some inner GPS system. He gets exactly where he needs to go, daylight or dark. I have to admit it, Fole is tough. Maybe if I tromped around with an ugly old troll in the dark more often, he would toughen me up too.

Finally, the lake appeared. Eric's nerves went from mildly jumpy to almost berserk. He saw evil eyes floating about the water's surface. He tapped Fole on the shoulder and whispered. *Alligators!*

Fole nodded.

In the starlight, the lake sparkled and looked kind of magical. Eric had no idea how long this boat scheme would take, but from what he'd gathered, these two wanted him to help Fole paddle the boat right into the middle of the lake and find the biggest lily pad blossom.

From there, Fole's instructions got fuzzier, mostly due to the language barrier. The troll understood him better than he could have imagined, but then he guessed trolls had observed (or maybe even made friends with?) people living in this forest a long time ago. Eric communicated OK, but it took lots of hand motions, and they were hard to see in the dark. Finally, Fole came up with a tiny stone to illustrate what it was he wanted Eric to find. For whatever reason, and Eric still couldn't guess the "why" of it, but Fole needed him to reach inside this flower to get his shiny pebble back out. *Whoever heard of hiding a pebble inside a flower? And how had Fole, with his short chubby arms, put it in there in the first place? Especially if he didn't swim with alligators, and he didn't have a boat! Or maybe Fole had already borrowed his dad's boat, without anyone knowing about it.*

Eric was not sure, but he had his rifle, the flashlight, and the boat, so...what the heck. He was here, and he couldn't turn back now. In his heart he knew he owed Fole something for shooting his pet. Besides, down deep in his gut, he was feeling kinda proud of himself. Finding a wild troll for a friend was pretty amazing, even for a soft city kid like him.

But, Eric, you could have killed his pet or yourself that day. You just wanted to show off to tell Jerry Lee. There went his conscience again. *Anyhow, I'm making up for it now, and won't Jerry Lee love hearing about this wacky adventure...if we live through it, that is.*

The plan seemed simple. Eric would paddle the boat, and Fole would be ready with the clubs, just in case an alligator got too close to the boat. Fole instructed Troelina to stay put in the bottom of the boat and not get in their way.

He still didn't understand why Fole had to be out here so late— unless he was afraid Ed wouldn't let Eric take the boat. Still, it would be way easier to find Fole's pebble in the daylight.

Eric had, in fact, already posed that question to Fole.

Unfortunately, Fole, like the stubborn little beast that he was, had replied, "Naagh." Case closed.

Chapter 18

IT BEGINS

Lilac Lake appeared serene under the soft moonlight. At the meeting hands of midnight, the water's glasslike surface began popping open. Out came little ripples of color, circling round and round, blending one into the other. The popping went on and on, like a boiling pot, until the entire lake turned its magical lilac hue.

In an instant, Garr appeared, his feathers shimmering white. Eric gasped. "There it is," he whispered. "The white thing is here."

Fole started paddling, straight toward the lily, a low growl simmering in his chest. Troelina shook in fear. Her two front feet clutched the side of the boat while her eyes searched the shoreline for goats.

Eric paddled, but his eyes would not focus on anything but the swan. In a hold-your-breath-slow motion, they moved ahead, the only other sound being the drips from the paddles as they dipped in and then back out again.

From opposite ends of the lake, both the swan and the rowboat advanced toward the middle. Neither noticed the little neon lights glowing in and around the giant lily at the lake's center stage. The roach bugs formed their battle stations.

Troelina groaned. "Naagh seasick." She lay down in the bottom of the boat.

Only the delicate white blossom was unaware there was drama ahead.

Garr lowered his magnificent beak, his strong neck curved in the shape of a harp. He skimmed along the water, quiet, confident, ready.

Troelina panicked. Her insides came upward, and she actually barfed. The smell was horrible. The presence of this strange white swan meant trouble; she could feel it. Besides that, she'd not sighted a single goat, which made her even more nervous. Surely, the goats knew by now that Fole was here and that he would help break her curse. Where were they hiding? The enemy she could not see loomed bigger than the one right in front of her. Her color paled.

In a sudden forward fury, Garr attacked. He thrust his beak at Fole. Eric was pleased to see Fole held position, in spite of the boat being rocked sideways. Troelina yelped and drew herself all in to hide, which was probably a good thing. Her body would be better protected as she lay in the boat bottom like ballast.

Eric was now aware his amazing "white thing" was this beautiful swan. But somehow, the swan had become Fole's enemy. *OK, then.* He dropped to his knees, holding tightly to his paddle. It offered a bit of resistance to the sway of the boat. With this little bit of angle, he stroked his paddle hard, hoping to ram the swan's body with the point of the bow. It connected but didn't appear to do any damage. Garr's resulting rage touched off a hot anger inside Fole. As the boat and swan collided, Fole stood right up and delivered a punt-kick to Garr's chest.

Garr shook it off, circled, and came back toward Eric with cunning speed, his beak open wide. Eric did the only thing he could do: at the last minute, he dodged. The vicious beak hit the edge of his seat with a thud, and water sloshed up between the boat and Garr's body, soaking Eric's pants. Garr recoiled, moved ahead, and struck again at Fole. He shielded this blow the best he could with his paddle, but beak connected with bone, and Fole's shoulder split open. He yelped aloud as the blood spurted. Eric reached down and felt for the rifle, but kept his eyes on the swan. Garr swam off, circled about, and rammed them again. The boat actually rocked a bit closer toward the lily. Eric took advantage of the moment and resumed paddling.

"Fole, you OK?"

Fole grunted, squeezing his shoulder to stop the bleeding. He was staring at two pairs of red eyes closing in on their boat.

Yipes. Eric saw them too—alligator eyes. He promised himself, "No matter what, we stay inside this boat." He set his mind to reaching that lily pad, but when Garr caught up to them, he slammed them pretty hard from behind.

"Hang on Fole!" Eric screamed in disbelief, for the paddle Fole held flew up, out, and hit the water with a splat. The gators took off after it.

Eric paddled harder. Fole leaned over with his club poised in his good hand. He stretched the other arm out, trying to grab for the lost paddle. Garr recovered, swam in from the side, and sent the paddle skimming across the surface out of Fole's reach. The paddle connected with part of the lily plant waving underneath the water and stuck. It stayed there, bobbing up and down. The impact started a reaction as the roach bugs stirred. About a dozen roaches jumped onto the paddle, like a platoon of tiny soldiers, waiting for orders to open fire.

Fole sat down. With those roaches entering this fight, he needed to rethink his strategy. Eric didn't take time to think. Garr was coming closer, and Eric's heart was banging hard. He paddled with renewed determination, his eyes locked on the white blossom that held Fole's pebble.

Could they get there before the swan?

Chapter 19

UNFORESEEN

E d woke up in a sudden sweat. He got up to open the window and stubbed his toe on the rocking chair.

"Ugh." He groaned and limped down the hall to the kitchen, reaching up to get his flashlight from the top of the refrigerator. It wasn't there.

Great; probably in Eric's room. Never mind. He was fully awake now. He flipped on the kitchen light, got an ice pack from the freezer, and sat down to attend his throbbing toe.

He heard the shed door banging. He sighed. *Eric must not have shut it tight.*

He tossed the ice bag in the sink, slipped into his moccasins, and started out the back door. *Flashlight?*

Back to Eric's room he went, but...what? No Eric. He checked his watch. It was after eleven. *Why is Eric in the shed...at this hour?*

Ed went out the back door, crossed the drive, and flipped the shed light on. *No.* Worse than that, his brain informed him, the rowboat was gone!

Ed panicked. He ran back to the house, forgetting his toe, and grabbed the truck keys. If Eric had taken off at this time of night, with the boat, then that Jerry Lee must be in on it. He suddenly remembered the way they'd grinned when he came into the room the last time Jerry Lee was here. And later, when he asked Eric what the secrecy was about, Eric had changed the subject. Those boys were up to something, and Ed intended to find out what. Something must be going down.

Elsa. He retraced his steps, leaving a hurried note on the counter: *Gone to pick up Eric. Don't worry.* He put the truck in neutral and rolled down the incline before starting the engine. *No sense waking her.*

Ed covered the few miles to Jerry Lee's in a few minutes and was shocked to realize the house was totally dark. *Had Jerry Lee snuck out too?*

Ed had no choice. He pounded on the door, waited a few seconds, and pounded again. He heard Snake, Jerry Lee's hound dog, growling on the other side. In a few minutes, Bob commanded, "Lie down!"

The door opened and he was inside. He apologized, explained, and waited while Bob took a bed check. He returned with a sleepy-eyed Jerry Lee stumbling behind him. Ed's nerves imploded.

"Do you have any idea why Eric would take my boat out at this hour, alone?" he asked, his voice pitching up.

"No, suh," replied Jerry Lee groggily. But then, in afterthought, he added, "Unless he went out huntin' for that white thang…but why would he, without tellin' me?"

"What 'white thing' would that be?"

"Umm, he's been sightin' this big white thang down round the lake. I tole him it was probably jes' a wood stork or somethin', but Eric thought he might go huntin' after it. I tole him if he went, he should call me tuh go with him…"

"Well, son, put on some clothes. We've got to go find him."

Bob and Jerry Lee got ready, and Ed was grateful to have them along. Bob had been educated in the north, but he knew this forest area better than anyone. Jerry Lee debated bringing the dog but decided against it. Snake had a tendency to howl at everything that moved, so they left him behind to guard the house.

The boat launch was at the end of Steenrod Road, but they reasoned Eric wouldn't have dragged the boat all that way around. It would be a shorter distance for him to go through the trees to get the boat straight into water. So they turned around and suddenly, Ed hit the brakes. A large goat stood in the middle of the road. Ed beeped the horn. The darned thing wouldn't move a single step.

Jerry Lee jumped out, waving his arms and hollering. The stubborn goat stayed glued to the spot. Jerry Lee climbed back in and Ed dropped it into first gear. Slowly, with bright lights glaring, they moved toward him, inch by inch. When the truck sidled up to within a foot, the foolish goat turned around, kicked up his back feet, and took off running—right down the middle of the road!

"Do ya b'lieve it?" said Jerry Lee. "I ain't never seen no goat act thataway. Do ya s'pose it got the rabies er somethin'?"

"I doubt that," said Bob, "But he is acting strange."

Ed rounded the next bend and came upon the rest of the herd. The whole lot of them stood stock still, blocking the road and staring blankly into his headlights.

"OK, hang on; we'll turn around and take the cut-off road. When we get closer, we'll head in on foot, OK?"

"I'm with ya," said Jerry Lee, "and don't worry. Eric knows about gators n' all, cuz we talked about it."

"That's good, but I'll admit it, I'm worried. I mean, this isn't like him to take off so late, without saying anything to anybody."

Ed pulled over and left the keys under the mat, just in case they got separated. Entering the woods, the three of them spread out a few feet apart and started walking in the direction of Lilac Lake. Jerry Lee kept his coon-hunter's headlamp in front of his face, beaming the way. They scanned the weeds and grass, checking for footprints or any sign the boat had recently been dragged through here.

The dashboard clock read 11:57 p.m. After covering maybe ten yards, they took turns hollering out Eric's name.

No answer came.

Chapter 20

STRUGGLE

E ric felt his neck bulge from the strain of paddling. He gave it his all, and they were getting closer, when something burned inside his upper arm. He looked down and saw a glowing bug. *Ouch!* It got him again. He sucked in the pain. He wouldn't put down his paddle. *I'm too close now.*

Fole sniffed as they neared the fragrant blossom. By sheer luck they were closer to the plant now than the swan. If only they could keep that vicious beak at bay a few more minutes.

"Hey what?" yelled Eric, pulling with all his might. He yanked at the paddle held fast beneath the water. Eric pulled up again, but the paddle wouldn't give. "Fole," he yelled, "The paddle's stuck...help me pull!"

Fole moved over. He placed his good hand on the paddle, and together, they yanked. Eric got another quick glimpse of Garr, who was barreling toward them. Eric wanted to keep at least one large floating lily pad leaf between him and the swan's beak. Each leaf from this humungous lily pad was as big and round as a hula hoop, and they were tough. Garr was big, but he couldn't stretch his neck out quite that far. Eric's maneuver around the leaves bought them a few extra seconds.

Fole held on. Eric slapped at his stings. Again, he reached down for the rifle, and just as he got a hold of it, several more bugs crawled up his neck. He felt them bite, twice, just under his jawline. *Ouch, hot!* Fole saw it happen, knew what it felt like even, but he was powerless to help. He kept working the paddle upward until finally, he made progress. Underneath the water's surface, the lily pad had sent out new growth. These narrow green tentacles wrapped themselves in and out like a pile of spaghetti. The paddle was tangled up there, and it held. Fole crouched down and slipped his bamboo blade from the water-pole tied around his waist. He sliced through the vines just as Garr hit them. Eric nearly toppled overboard. He was suffering now, crawling with roaches on his chest and his stomach.

Finally, the paddle came free. Fole growled. He was also getting stung again. He swung the paddle out in a fury, one armed, with a long right hook. It caught Garr square on the temple of his sparkling, elegant head. Stunned, Garr blinked, but he didn't move.

"Steady," said Eric. He leaned way over, grabbing onto the blossom. His stomach burned like crazy. He held one petal and reached inside with his other hand to feel around…was that it? Fole's pebble?

In the same instant, Eric watched Garr come barreling in after Fole. His hand slipped away from the blossom as an unexplained shadow swooped down from the trees. Everybody looked up. A mockingbird? She flew neatly in between them, slipped her beak inside that delicate blossom, and plucked the pearl out, just as slick as you please. Then up she flew again, beating her wings hard to avoid their wrath. She held it in her beak like a prized blueberry. Over them all she flew, holding on tight.

The mockingbird stole it. Eric could only stare. Fole was speechless; that is, until he watched that horrid bird open up her beak. She was almost over the swan's head and she just…let it go. She purposely dropped it. Down the pearl spiraled, in a time-delayed sparkle, like the shimmering drops of a July Fourth fireworks display. Her piercing cackle ripped through the darkness, sounding like a witch bubbling up a new brew.

Eric wanted to cry. After all that, she had been waiting there, watching them struggle, and then she flew right above the swan at the final, plucking moment! Fole screamed. His head dropped to his chest, and his eyes scrunched tight.

"Hey, Fole, wait, look—he *missed* it!" Eric hollered. He stared in shock again at the tiny circle of ripples, now spreading outward from a single circle near Garr's beak. Garr jerked his head underwater, beak open, trying to recover the precious pearl from the spot where it hit the water. But it sunk. Sunk! Garr's beak fell open, unable to believe it. His precious transforming potion, gone! Fole's shiny pebble, lost! Poor Troelina's magic curse-breaking pearl…disappeared! Down into the lilac water…forever. No, actually, not forever. For according to the ancient legends, another magic pearl could blossom there, but it could take a hundred years.

But there was no time to do anything about it. Eric heard shouting in the distance.

"Eric, where are you?" He gulped. *His father.* He pointed to the opposite shore and Fole sprang into action.

Get out of here, light speed.

Chapter 21

BUSTED!

As fast as they could, Eric and Fole paddled away from Garr and the shouting voices. The little boat rocked, but there was no time to worry if Garr was following or what to do about Fole's lost pebble or even Eric's stinging, itchy bites…no. They reached the shore, and Fole lifted Troelina out onto the bank. She stuck her head out briefly, her color still a pale sickly yellow. "Troelina naagh good," she mumbled. "Pukey." She looked down at her feet and got swoony seasick again. Fole jumped out after her, tossed his paddle in, and helped Eric pull till the boat was secured.

"Troelina, come," Fole said, pointing to the trees with his good arm.

Eric was getting sick, too—dizzy and nauseous. He didn't protest when Fole spread him flat to the ground and began smearing his neck and chest with cold, wet sand and soggy leaves. Instead he tried to ignore the itch and stare up at the moon. Bright stars twinkled over his head. "Bloomin' unbelievable troll," he murmured as he felt his heart slow to a more normal beat. He closed his eyes.

"Eric! Where are you, Eric?"

His father was coming. Eric's eyes popped open. *Fole?*

"*Go!*" whispered Eric, pointing to the forest. "Fole, go now."

Fole winced in pain, but he muscled the clubs and Troelina up tight under his arms. He slipped away under cover of the trees just as Eric's father, Jerry Lee, and Bob stepped out of the woods.

Oh no. The rifle was still in the boat. It was Eric's turn to wince, but he knew there might also be an alligator lurking somewhere within striking distance. With that in mind, it was better to make lots of noise so Dad could find him. He was really going to catch it; he knew that. He'd probably be grounded till old age because of this. But he took away one comfort: he hadn't wimped out, not once. The creepy-weird things that drew him out here might command the dark, but they wouldn't win. He wasn't afraid anymore, and holy bleepin' crap-ola, did he ever have some wild stuff to tell Jerry Lee now.

"I'm over here," he yelled and then thought, *Yes, I am here, jes' like a reg'lar southern hunter boy. Heck, if I could ruh-member the words, ah'd be singin' "Dixie" myself tonight.* He propped himself up on one elbow and stared at the trees, wondering how far Fole would get before stopping for the night. He worried about his shoulder. He also wondered if he and the swan would fight again. What was losing the special pebble going to mean to them, when morning came? Clearly, there was way more happening out here than he knew. *I can't wait to find out all the details...why was that swan going after us, anyway?*

Eric eyed the water again for the swan. Where had he gone? Was he going after Fole? He could hear footsteps coming toward him.

Look now how the water color is all changed back to normal...so strange. He wondered how the lake had turned colors—or had it all been his imagination? Eric lifted his head and felt dizzy again. The cool sand felt better on his burning skin. Right now, all he wanted was to go home and sleep. Somehow he had to get rid of this itchiness that was making him feel so horrible.

"Dad," he called out. A flashlight beam bobbed in his direction. In big trouble or not, he would be home soon. Eric closed his eyes, his stomach churning.

He was busted.

Chapter 22

SOLUTION

Ed, Bob, and Jerry Lee loaded Eric and the boat into the back of the pickup. Fole and Troelina hid themselves under a fallen log, not too far from where Troelina had dug her second tunnel exit. Fole carried her the whole way. When he set her down, he coaxed her out of her shell. She looked worn out, but she didn't vomit.

"Troelina naagh ride boat, naagh evermore," she vowed. Her eyes filled with tearful questions as she looked searchingly at Fole.

Fole breathed deep. He had to tell her about losing the pearl. It wasn't coming easy. He launched into the account, giving her the awful details of what took place while she'd been sick inside her shell. Fole admitted his failure in not reaching the magic pearl before the mockingbird snatched it up.

"Er-rinck hepp Fole," he said. "Er-rinck aaghgood." He knew she was unhappy, but he did not allow her to voice too much drama about it.

"Troelina…what is, what is," he said, his voice final. Fole looked into her eyes. "Fole love Troelina, evermore," he said. He would figure something out.

Troelina slowly turned herself around in a small circle, dragging her injured leg. Again, she cried, but not from the pain, because even though her leg was tender and swollen, it had stopped bleeding hours ago. She knew it would heal. Her tears fell because her heart hurt, and that was huge.

"Naagh together, Fole. See Troelina so...so tortoise." Her tears started again but Fole held her while she sobbed. When she calmed down, he scooped out a hole in the sand, lined it with leaves and placed her tenderly in it.

"Stay," he commanded. He placed her club beside her, although he doubted she could even lift it now.

Fole had been thinking. He grabbed his club and stood up.

"Fole naagh go," she sniffled.

"Goatsland," he said with a slight growl.

"Naagh Fole. Naagh Goatsland."

"Fole go. Troelina stay." He started off, looking back only once.

Whatever troll would do, Fole would do; Troelina knew this deep in her heart. But her mind didn't like it.

The doves had begun to coo, and the sun would soon burst up.

"Oh, my Fole," she said. As tired as she was, Troelina would not pull herself in until Fole returned safely beside her.

She could only wait, eyes alert and heart aflutter.

Chapter 23

REVENGE GOATSLAND

Fole moved fast. Upon arriving in Goatsland this time, he refused to hide himself. Instead, he saw three female goats grazing in the morning dew and made it a point to growl menacingly at each of them. He wanted Krug to know he'd arrived on his turf.

He munched a sweet tangerine and made sure to walk where he would leave a solid trail. When he found the right place, he sat down to wait. In time, the mean old goat would come after him, and when he did, Fole would be ready. He only hoped that when Krug came down upon him, those disgusting roaches would be busy glowing elsewhere.

Fole didn't wait long. He heard the sound of goat hooves striking the ground before he caught their movement. Several females milled around beyond a patch of bamboo to his left, but they kept their distance, regarding him with wild, wary eyes.

Suddenly, Krug pranced out alone to greet the intruder. He stood there, looking hard at Fole as if he might butt him clear to Jupiter.

Fole sat very still. Krug circled slowly around him. Fole said nothing. Krug suddenly smiled his most evil smile. He noted with quiet glee that Fole sat upon the exact circle where Troelina had been cursed. He had easily made her disappear inside the spinning tunnel, and so far as he could tell, there was no reason not to do the same for this frumpy-lump of troll. Oh yes, Krug was going to have his own kind of fun today.

It was Fole who broke the silence. "Goat's roaches," he said.

"Indeed," Krug replied with a sneer. "Did they give you a bad time? Certainly you trolls must know better than to trespass where you do not belong."

"Curse Troelina?" he asked. Fole grinned then, too, in an almost friendly way.

"Hail that, I did. The sassy little tramp will live on the ground forever for her rude ways. And so might you, if you don't kiss the goat's ground you rest upon, right now." Krug lowered his head.

"Naagh," declared Fole, raising his club.

Krug's straggly beard almost touched the ground. His eyes expanded to lime size.

"No troll *ever* faces me without doing as I say," Krug declared in his raspy voice. He moved a step closer.

Fole sat like a mushroom. He stared back at the goat, not flinching so much as an eyelash.

In a sudden rage, Krug jumped right at him, whispering the dreaded curse words that opened up the ground. Down Fole slid!

"Aagh Troelina, the Fole be cursed," hollered Fole, laughing triumphantly as he spiraled dizzily through the eerie darkness. No matter, Krug. In one form or another, Fole would be with his Troelina for now and evermore.

Krug was taken aback. "Silly slobberhead trolls," he bellowed. He thought for a moment. Perhaps he could have used a different curse. Maybe it would have been better to make this belligerent troll smell like a skunk for all his days. But then, the whole goat herd had been watching. Both of those stubborn purple trolls were now totally removed from his special pasture space; so the dirty deed was done.

"StanzeGreegan Fooh. Goats rule!" he proclaimed, and with his ego fluffed fine and fancy, he rounded up his followers.

"Trolls be cursed," he declared and marched his herd off to the uppermost stream, where they would drink in Krug's celebration.

Chapter 24

SUFFERING SWAN

In a state of acute distress, Garr circled the spot where the mocking-bird dropped the pearl down to him. How could he have missed it? He swam back and forth, again and again, reliving the horrid moment, as if that alone could undo the damage.

Inside his head, Garr heard his father saying, "It's all up to you." The pride he held inside his chest melted with the loss of the pearl. Lilac Lake had soaked him to his core. No swan nesting ritual now, perhaps ever. No clutch of shiny silver eggs and no royal heir. He had failed his own kind.

In a curious way, however, he felt his father would understand. Garr wanted the pearl, but only from his own egotistical pride. Now that he'd be a source of historical embarrassment, his biggest dilemma was this: "What should I do about it now? How important is this royalty stuff to me, after all?"

Garr had prepared only to win. He didn't understand what it would mean if he lost. The swan generations coming after him would wear no royal label. He swam around muttering to himself, "Can they live without it?" Maybe he should stay here with the common swans for the rest of his days. Who would care, really? Who among them would even know? It was a beautiful lake and he loved being a part of it. Or perhaps he should go away somewhere to hang his head in shame. *But, go? Go where?*

If he flew back to his father's world, he could not stay there—not among the dead. Garr watched the lake. Guarding it was his habit, and he no longer cared where the others went or what they did. Did it mean the mighty Garr was just a mighty loser? He slept on it. He took stock of himself. He was still a large, healthy swan. Would that—could that—be enough? Things might have ended differently. He'd been born a royal swan, but it did not make him untouchable. Once the boat had gotten between him and the huge lily plant, he simply lost his chance to grab for the pearl, although the bird tried to help him. He'd formed a new respect for mocking-birds and humans along with a new wariness of trolls. The truth was, Garr felt a little afraid for the first time in his life. Without his royal label to protect him or set him apart, poor Garr had lots to learn about fitting in with a normal flock. Did he possess the courage to try?

Back at Eric's house, Elsa tended to the roach bites on his pink, puffy skin. For the first time Eric could remember, she seemed quite upset about something other than dirt. She got angry over the way Eric's recklessness had worried them.

"I was upset to see your father so scared," she said, with tears in her eyes. And when they finally explained everything to her, she'd hugged him a long time. Her display of unexpected affection blew him away.

Ed restricted him to the house until they could talk things over. Eric knew his dad was fair, but he was also really mad. Eric decided he wouldn't argue or whine about it. At least he could heal before he was punished. His adventures had left him with amazing memories etched deep in his brain. *Whatever Dad's punishment is, it can't last forever, and I deserve it, right?*

So what if the rifle was taken away? Maybe he didn't even care anymore. He knew plenty of grown men who didn't have to shoot a gun or kill anything. He understood now. It didn't mean they were wimps.

Eric didn't have much more energy to think. The sharp painful memory of hurting the innocent tortoise would always be hard. It was someone his friend Fole cared an awful lot about. The tortoise hadn't asked for any of the pain it got. It was sorta like Eric finally faced down his own inside hurt by watching it happen from the outside. He hadn't asked for any of the pain he got either, not from the divorce. But the two people he loved the most, his mom and dad, gave him pain anyway, not because they wanted to hurt him but because their differences were real. Divorce? He had only two choices. He could accept it and all the changes it made to his life, like having Elsa in it. Or he could go on being miserable. Some hard choices just forced hard decisions.

Eric also kept thinking about that mockingbird. How had she known to come sneak the pebble right out from under their noses, so super-awesome slick? He smiled. He'd never forget that cackling sound, not in a gazillion years. He was sure looking forward to asking Fole a whole bunch of questions.

Now, though, his biggest urge was to scratch. He only hoped he could get to sleep before it drove him totally nuts.

In spite of having to stay home in bed a few days and getting into so much trouble and all, he was eager for Jerry Lee's next visit. The dumbfounded look on his skinny-smug face was something Eric couldn't wait to see.

What Eric did have to wait for was another visit from Fole and Troelina. Several weeks went by where night after night, Eric sat by his window, looking out and hoping to see them. He'd almost given up hope, until one afternoon he took out the trash and left the shed door open. He came back to close it and spied movement. He stopped and looked again. There. Not one but two gopher tortoises were sitting right up in the rowboat.

"Holy guacamole!" yelled Eric, dropping the garbage can in surprise. And, on the seat right beside them, lay his bolas.

"What the hey," he mumbled, and then heard a familiar command. "Err-rinck hepp Fole."

Eric's nose nearly jumped off his face. He stared, unable to speak.

"Aagh Err-inck, mybolass aaghgood."

"Fole?" he stammered. "Fole, is, is that really you?"

The larger tortoise nodded, smiling wide.

"But...Fole. How did you...um, why, er...how on earth did you...change yourself like that?"

Troelina laughed out loud in her funny, bubbly giggle.

"Lo-o-ove," she said, making goo-goo eyes at Fole.

"Err-rinck sit," said Fole, patting the seat and crossing his chubby front legs.

Eric sat.

"Aaghgood. Fole talk."

Epilogue

THE TROLL'S STORY

The story Fole told to Eric that day sounded a little like some mushy old TV rerun. You know, the kind of tale where boy meets girl, gets love struck, and then decides he can do anything to rescue her, even (in Fole's case, anyway) invite a goat curse upon his own body so he would be changed to match his girlfriend's species.

Except that Fole also shared more information about the troll's remaining tribe members. One by one, all the trolls he had left behind, without getting any word of Fole and Troelina's fate, had gathered up their collective courage. Like the stalwart friends they were, they banded together and stormed back into Goatsland to confront the evil Krug. As a tribe they demanded their friends be returned. As one can imagine, this invasion started up another huge troll and goat fight. In the end, however, there were way too many goats and not quite enough purple trolls. The whole lot of them (the trolls, that is) were cursed.

Krug didn't know it then, or maybe he didn't care, but cursing them all at once actually did a tremendous favor for the trolls. For purple trolls were more than endangered they were dying out. By using the turning curse against them and changing them all into gopher tortoises, the whole tribe would have at least a fighting chance to survive in today's world. (Should you ever hike through what is left of the deepest forest in Central Florida, to this very day, you may spot one, for these large land tortoises live on still, in happiness and harmony, bothering no one. Slowly, they go about their daily digs with good purpose.)

But geez, for Fole's sake, don't blab this news around, OK?

Who knows what kind of horrid experiments those humans might do, if they knew an ancient civilization of purple trolls thrived among them still, so well disguised?

After the astonishing night of lilac waters (as Eric now refers to it), he stayed home a lot. First, he had to do research to write a term paper required by his father as part of his punishment. He worked hard though and made it a good paper. He learned a lot reading Florida's history and all about the many wild animals living there. He kept his promise to Fole and Troelina—which meant he did not include the troll's real story in his paper. (Like, who would believe it anyway?)

Besides writing the paper, Ed made Eric enroll in (and pass) a gun safety class. He was then allowed to keep his .22 rifle. Jerry Lee went to class with him, and both agreed to join a shooting club and practice target shooting afterward.

Eric decided he might never become a true southern hunter, but, he reasoned, it wouldn't hurt if a guy had a few friends who were, right?

And talk about awesome luck. The following summer, Eric returned to Florida, without his mom insisting he do so. He had given her an almost-full rundown of his awesome experiences, and she agreed he could stay for the entire summer. Bob found him a job working in the Everglades. Jerry Lee was there too, and together they helped collect data on several endangered species, including gopher tortoises.

To be honest, Eric sometimes still gets quite annoyed at Jerry Lee's bragging. But he liked the 4-H club a lot and thought, maybe, he would consider raising a couple goats. He wouldn't have to eat them, but his mouth kinda started watering whenever Elsa made his favorite chocolate-peanut-butter goat's milk fudge—so why not?

Wait a second…what happened to the mean, old, evil Krug? As most everyone knows by now, goats and trolls have never gotten along well together. Once Krug discovered he had made all the trolls disappear from his forest, there was no one left for him to terrorize. Therefore, he trip-trap-trip-trapped his herd right on over the big river bridge, leading them further south and closer to the beach. Krug has not been heard from since that day, but this move turned out to be a grave mistake. Two horrible hurricanes later hit the coastal area and scattered his goats far and wide.

Without their evil leader to round them up, the goats simply wandered further away.

Most of those goats are now domesticated. Some (like Krug) may amuse themselves by butting their human caregivers or by chasing the chickens around down in Key West. (This latest information came by way of the squirrels, so there is no reason to doubt it.)

Oh, yes. Do not forget the mockingbird. One hates to stereotype, but mockingbirds continue to be rather gossipy creatures. They flit nosily about, attempting to mind everyone else's business.

As both the trolls and goats discovered, a mockingbird simply cannot be trusted and will cause malfunctions wherever it flies. Yet these birds do serve one good purpose. Mockingbirds sometimes gather to feed upon those ugly neon roaches. An extremely odd appetite to be sure, but it helps keep this nasty insect population in check.

All things considered, the wisest creatures among us will pay a mockingbird absolutely no attention.

The End

AUTHOR BIOGRAPHY

Wilma Fleming would love to hear any personal comments you have. Please visit her website, www.WilmaWrites.com, and feel free to leave a message.

Thank you for reading her first (but not last) novel, and if you enjoyed it, please add a short review on www.Amazon.com. Your input is truly valuable to this author.

To order more copies of *The Curse at Lilac Waters*, please go to https://www.createspace.com/. The book is available on Kindle.

Made in the USA
Middletown, DE
18 September 2017